STATES

of

EXILE

Dennis Jung

States of Exile

©2020 Dennis Jung

print ISBN: 978-1-09833-454-3

ebook ISBN: 978-1-09833-455-0

ALSO BY DENNIS JUNG

POTIONS (out of print)

STILL LIFE IN A RED DRESS

JACK OF ALL TRADES

THE MORNING OF THE WORLD

THE LANGUAGE OF THE DEAD

SIGNS OF LIFE

THE ANGEL'S CHAIR

ACKNOWLEDGEMENTS

There are two sources whose contributions were critical in the research required in the writing of this novel. First, **"Days of the Fall"**, Jonathan Spyer's accounts of his reporting on the Syrian and Iraqi wars provided invaluable background for these conflicts. **"The Battle for the Mountain of the Kurds"** by Thomas Schmidinger offered insights into Kurdish history and their struggle for autonomy.

I would like to express my gratitude to my friends Sara and Erin for their editing assistance and providing further suggestions, and to my wife Kathleen for her support and critiques.

I should also credit and offer my appreciation to Lynsey Addario, the renowned American photojournalist, for her unwitting contribution in often serving as the template for my character Harper Harris.

Finally, I should thank the Google God for its invaluable contribution to my research. With Google's help I was able to consult untold numbers of articles, accounts, maps, films and photographs that helped in my attempts to capture and describe a part of the world of which I had no firsthand experience.

Dedicated to all those who must flee for life or love.

STATES *of* EXILE

PREFACE

The United Nations High Commissioner for Refugees has estimated that by the end of 2018 there were over 70 million people worldwide that had been forced from their homes by conflict or persecution. Among them are 30 million refugees, over half of whom are under the age of eighteen. As a result of the Syrian Civil War, 5.6 million Syrians have fled their country since 2011. Another 6.2 million have been displaced within their own country. Again, half of these refugees are children.

Refugees, unlike migrants, have seen their lives violently altered by repression or war. They lose their homes, their livelihoods, even their loved ones. And as they are forced to flee, they enter into a cruel contract where they exchange dignity for simple survival. And too often in the process, they encounter humanity at its worst.

In our nation's current socio-political climate, many of our fellow citizens see immigrants and refugees as a threat to our values. But what values will there be to uphold if we abandon our duty to protect those less fortunate than ourselves, human beings who have fled their homes due to misfortune not wholly of their own making. We must ask ourselves what incentives can we provide these people to assimilate into the fabric of our society if that fabric is so tattered that we are blind to the suffering of others. If our society is unable to welcome them, if we are unable to hold up to them an image of a better life, then how can we expect them to accept that our world is a better one than the one they fled?

The refugees in this story, while not the main actors in this drama, provide a backdrop for the personal stories of my characters. The refugee crisis is an off-screen presence that cannot be ignored. The character of Harper Harris who has served as the protagonist in three of my previous novels, sees herself as a witness, a recorder of how the world works; its tragedies and its ugliness as well as its beauty and wonder. She considers it her duty to bear witness for those people and places that are otherwise forgotten by our society's tendency to both trivialize and sensationalize the plight of the world and those less fortunate than ourselves. We live in a culture where the five o'clock news has already faded from our consciousness by the time the first reality show or sitcom begs for our vapid attention.

For my readers who are familiar with my trilogy of novels that feature Ms. Harris, you may be pleased that I chose to continue the arc of her story. The inspiration for this tale, like so many of my other novels, came about in an unlikely manner. In this case, a visit to a retrospective photo exhibit featuring the work of a renowned Slovenian photojournalist at the National Museum of Contemporary History in Ljubljana. It led me to delve more deeply into the history of the Balkan Wars of the 1990s. In the first Harper Harris novel, *Still Life in a Red Dress,* she alludes to her time spent covering that tragic conflict. Thus, I chose to begin this story with a lecture and a retrospective exhibit of her career. From there, the story unfolds on a surprising trajectory that leads her to Kurdistan and northern Iraq, an area rife with refugees. I realized that crisis would have to become a player in this story, albeit in a secondary role.

For Harper Harris, everything is about the story, much to the dismay of her agent, therapist, and her adopted daughter. Thus, she somewhat unwillingly sets out on an ill-advised but tempting odyssey filled with the usual dangerous mishaps, but also the connections and revelations that compose her story. I hope you enjoy reading it as much as I enjoyed writing it.

Santa Fe, August 2020

PART ONE

What has become of the adventures of the heart?
Killed by the dark adventures of existence."
-Erich Maria Remarque

1

NATIONAL MUSEUM OF
CONTEMPORARY HISTORY
LJUBLJANA, SLOVENIA
NOVEMBER 19TH, 2019

Harper Harris gazed out the window of the museum's lecture hall at the approaching dusk and the bare, mist-shrouded chestnut trees. According to her host, an earnest young woman from STA, the Slovenian Press Agency, the weather had been unseasonably warm and sunny until an overnight cold front gifted the city with a light dusting of snow. Harper watched as a troop of people in identical yellow rain slickers emerged ghost-like from the trees and scurried toward a waiting tour bus. A Japanese tourist group, she guessed, gauging from the calligraphy signage on the front of the bus and the flowery Oriental motif of their open umbrellas.

Harper had rather impulsively agreed to the lecture and retrospective photo exhibition six months earlier, before her energy had been sapped by her recent assignment in Syria. Reneging on the commitment had never been an option, for the advance fee was immediately consumed by her adopted daughter Funaya's fall tuition at the overpriced boarding school in upstate New York. Her ambivalence about traveling to Ljubljana had been tempered by her curiosity in seeing the city she had last visited in 1991, back when the threat of a war in the Balkans was merely a vague possibility. At the time, the city had been awash in the exuberance over its recent and unexpected independence from the disintegrating Yugoslav Republic. Little did anyone know that the heady times the Slovenians enjoyed foretold the bloody days ahead for their restless neighbor republics to the south.

On that visit, she had been accompanied by a young Frenchman, a journalist with Le Monde, who the following year would fall victim to a sniper's bullet in the opening days of the Serbian invasion of Croatia. Rene was his name, and he had briefly been her lover, their dalliance interrupted by a mutual ennui as much as a bullet.

Her memories of those days in Ljubljana consisted mostly of wine-soaked interviews with jubilant students in the sidewalk cafes along the river that intersected the city's old quarter. Her only other visit had been a two hour layover at the airport on her way to Sarajevo.

"Pardon me, Miss Harris," a voice behind her interrupted her thoughts. It was the young woman from the press agency. Her short, purple-streaked hair, liver-colored lipstick and nose ring seemed in sharp contrast with the severe, black pantsuit she wore over a frilly white blouse. "The lights," she said, pointing up at the ceiling, "You must tell me. They are perhaps too bright?"

Harper glanced first up at the chandeliered ceiling and then at the two dozen or so rows of chairs, most of which were already occupied. Another fifty or so people stood lined along the exquisitely ornate, Venetian plastered walls of the small lecture hall.

"No, they're fine for now. You can dim them when I start the photos."

Harper scanned the audience for any familiar faces, but failed to recognize anyone. She had hoped to see at least some acquaintance, a fellow correspondent perhaps. Most of the audience seemed middle-aged or older except for the entire front row which was occupied by what appeared to be high school or college students.

"Shall I begin the introduction?" her host asked.

Harper nodded and strolled over to the podium and began fiddling with her laptop as the young woman began her introduction in Slovenian. Harper tapped a key and an image appeared on the screen behind the podium.

It was her first published photograph; an image of a slender middle-aged black woman leaning on a shovel in front of what appeared to be a wire chicken coop. The woman's broad smile and bright eyes hinted at the sensual allure that undoubtedly persuaded the white farmer for whom she once share-cropped to trade the deed for a hundred acres of prime bottom land for her favors. Harper's mother had spoken to her only once about the night Harper was conceived, and then in only the vaguest terms. Oddly enough, her mother's recounting seemed tinged with more warmth than regret.

She clicked off the laptop, and as she waited for her host to finish, she glanced over at the large gilded mirror on the side wall. The reflection of the woman standing by the podium was that of a trim, middle-aged, caramel-complexioned woman dressed in an ankle-length turquoise-colored skirt, a waist-length black leather jacket, and a scarlet head scarf that partially concealed her stylishly-cut mop of red hair. Anyone able to study her face more closely would undoubtedly notice the resemblance with the woman who had once posed before the chicken coop; the same generous mouth, the high forehead, and the deep set eyes, the irises that would appear coppery in the right light.

"Miss Harris," the host now intoned in English, "is the recipient of numerous awards, including two Pulitzer Prizes. Her work has been featured many times in National Geographic magazine, and her photographs have been exhibited in more museums than I could possibly list. Her reporting on many of the world's conflicts has also won her numerous journalism awards. Her byline has been featured in many of the world's leading magazines and newspapers. Please let us welcome Harper arrisharris."Harris."

The audience broke into polite, lengthy applause that Harper finally cut short with a wave of her hands. "Please. You're too kind. It has been too long since I've been to your lovely city," she said, nodding her head. "1991 to be exact. Those were exciting times for Slovenians." A soft murmur erupted from the audience and someone in the rear of the hall clapped. "That particular visit meant so much to me. You see, at the time I was a relatively inexperienced journalist. And this was to be my first major newspaper assignment."

She paused to collect her thoughts. She never enjoyed public speaking; never had overcome the awkwardness of discussing her work on such a personal level. When pressed as to why, she deflected by confessing that it was really more the subject matter of many of her photos that caused her unease. She lifted her gaze to the glittering chandelier above her for a moment before continuing.

"Sadly enough, the tragedies that overcame your neighbors to the south gave me my first break. It launched a career that has taken me to far more places than I could have ever imagined growing up on a small farm in the American South. The lights, please," she said and clicked on the first image.

"1979. This is my mother on her farm. She bought me my first camera, and the rest is history you might say," she said. She hesitated a few seconds before advancing to the next image.

"Some of you perhaps may recognize this one."

The grainy black and white photo depicted a group of jubilant young men and women clutching wine bottles and clinging to a large statue of a winged dragon. "Your city. June, 1991." Several members of the audience broke into applause. "Is there anyone here this evening who might be in that picture?" she asked, breaking into a grin. "No? Well gauging from the number of wine bottles, your lack of memory can be forgiven."

The audience responded with polite laughter. She clicked again and an image appeared of a pair of black women standing in a muddy road hemmed in on either side by thick forest. One of the women cradled a nude infant in her arms; the other woman's arms encircled a large straw basket, their faces registering nothing more than numbness born of what seemed fatigue and despair.

"The Congo, 1996. These women were fleeing the war."

She looked back at the audience. "Someone once asked me why I take photos. I told them I take photographs so I can remember. To flesh out my life. That's why any of us take photos. Right? We wish to remember the joys these images represent, but also we want to be reminded of the bittersweet." She paused for a few seconds before going on. "And some of us take photographs to document the pain we can't turn away from. When I look at my work I realize that some of my photos are true. Some hit the mark so to speak. And some do not. Tonight I will show you photos that hit the mark. At least they do that for me. They mean something to me," she said, placing her palm to her chest. "These photos are very personal. In fact, some of them are from my private collection and have never been published or exhibited. And then there are photos that I will not show for they are too personal, too painful."

She went to the next photo. It was a stark image of a coiled hand protruding from beneath the white sand of what one assumed was a beach. In the background, and slightly out of focus, was an elderly man clutching a hoe of some sort and squatting at the foot of a ragged palm tree.

"2004. The aftermath of the Indonesian tsunami. My first Pulitzer," she said solemnly. "The old man in the background found out later that the hand belonged to his daughter." She went on to the next one.

"This was taken in 2008 in Darfur near one of the refugee camps."

It was an odd image of a bearded Caucasian man apparently attempting to block her camera with his hand. In the background one could just make out what appeared to be a pile of burning bundles, garbage perhaps. One would have to look closely to recognize the bundles were actually bodies. Not able to help herself, she stared at the image for a long moment. Darfur was the first time she met Sonny Day. She had followed him to Nicaragua for the sake of a story. When it became more than a story, she lost him. The word was he died in a car accident in Cuba. She lingered on the image for longer than was necessary before going on to the next.

"2009. Managua, Nicaragua. This woman is one of many forced to forage in these garbage dumps simply in order to exist."

The image was that of an old woman sifting through a smoldering mountain of garbage, the sky in the background a blood red canvas. Newsweek had paid her handsomely for that shot and the accompanying essay, and to her everlasting shame, she spent all of it renting a condo in Maui while licking her wounds. She moved on to the next one.

"1995. Srebrenica, Bosnia."

An audible gasp erupted from some of the audience as a black and white image revealed a muddy ditch littered with hundreds of bodies sprawled in grotesque repose, their limbs entangled. She paused, at a loss of what else to say. A long moment of silence passed before she moved to the next photo.

It showed a woman with long, dirty blonde hair and wearing a patch over her left eye, her face partially in shadow. She was leaning over a candle, a tin cup in one hand, a cigarette in the other, and laughing.

"This was taken in Aleppo, Syria. 2012. My friend, the correspondent Marie Colvin. She was killed a month later in Homs." Harper stared at the photo for a moment before going on to the next image.

"I took this next photo shortly afterwards. I was part of a small group attempting to flee the fighting in Syria to safety over the mountains into Lebanon."

The photo showed two women seated on a fallen tree trunk, their faces downcast. One could assume they were Muslim from the *hijab* visible beneath their heavy wool head scarves. A small child at their feet appeared to be pushing a toy car along the muddy path.

"I took this photo several minutes before we were captured by Syrian troops. The woman on the left, the child's grandmother, was killed by Syrian soldiers a mere fifteen minutes or so after this photo was taken. I never found out the fate of the other woman and her child."

A black and white image appeared next showing a bare stony field surrounded by a forest of listless gray palm trees. It always took a moment for the observer to realize the white stones were arranged in linear rows. One of the stones in the foreground was surrounded by a clutch of small, colored bottles and a bouquet of wilted flowers.

"This was also taken in 2012 outside of a village in Liberia, West Africa. A graveyard for the victims of the war," she said simply. "Two years later, I was back in West Africa to cover the Ebola outbreak in Sierra Leone."

She clicked the next photo. It was a close up shot of Funaya as she stood in the gateway of the orphanage outside of Freetown. It was difficult to tell if the look on her face reflected surprise or anxious uncertainty. Harper moved to the next one without comment.

"Freetown, Sierra Leone. This is a… Well, I hesitate to call it a hospital. It was more like a hospice for the victims of Ebola. A young Belgian nurse working there very appropriately called it God's Waiting Room."

She had interviewed the nurse as she washed the blood and feces-stained linens in the muddy stream behind the hospital. Harper heard later that she had contracted Ebola and had been airlifted home. Whether she survived Harper never found out.

The picture revealed the shadowy interior of what might have once been a warehouse gauging from what appeared to be loading docks and chains with pulleys suspended from the rafters. The floor appeared haphazardly littered with cots, some draped in mosquito netting, others empty. Several of the empty ones appeared marked with some kind of stain. Other than a solitary nun standing in the foreground, the picture was devoid of anyone not confined to the cots.

"I must apologize for some of my choices of photos. Some of them are quite grim. What can I say? We live in a world where it is increasingly difficult to look away from tragedy." She glanced down at her laptop. "How about I show something lighter? This is my daughter Funaya in her bedroom in New York."

It showed a lanky adolescent girl with skin the color of Belgian chocolate sprawled on her unmade bed, encircled by a half-dozen open books. Her broad face registered a feigned horror. "Studying for her mid-term exams.. Still too grim," she added with a laugh before moving on to the next image.

"1995. What was referred to as Sniper Alley during the siege of Sarajevo."

A black and white image of two people, a man and a woman lying side by side in the street in a pool of blood.

"They were said to be lovers. The woman fell wounded and her lover was shot while attempting to drag her to safety. He was Serbian Christian Orthodox. The woman was a Bosnian Muslim."

"Again, 1995, Drina River, Bosnia."

A color image of a group of soldiers dressed in mismatched camouflage standing in a semicircle, in the center of which stood a tall, rangy man dressed in crisp fatigues and notable for the powder blue beret he wore at a jaunty angle. What appeared to be a small US flag was affixed to his sleeve. In contrast to the men surrounding him, he bore no obvious weapons. His right arm was extended in what appeared to be defiance in the direction of a huge, bearded man wearing crisscrossed bandoliers and holding a handgun aloft as if in celebration. Only then, did one's eyes take in the figure of a young man kneeling between them, his hands folded behind his head.

"My colleagues and I came upon this UN observer bartering with the Serbian militia for the release of a captured Bosnian Muslim."

"Do you remember his name?" a woman's voice suddenly shouted from somewhere in the audience.

"What?" Harper stammered, taken aback by this unexpected query. She squinted into the audience as she tried to locate her interrogator.

"The UN soldier in the blue beret. What was his name?"

The woman's accent sounded Middle European, German perhaps. Harper could vaguely make out the figure in one of the rear rows, but her face was in too much shadow to be discernible. Harper stared at the woman in confusion. The audience, sensing her unease, swiveled their gaze back and forth between the woman and Harper.

She had included the photo at the last moment, grappling with the dormant emotions it aroused. Now her sudden regret for including it left her struggling for a response. Of course, I know his name, Harper thought to herself. She glanced back at the screen, still fumbling for a reply.

"No. I don't recall his name. It was a long time ago," she said, finally.

There was a moment of silence before the woman abruptly stood and pushed her way past her fellow audience members before turning and making her way to the exit doors. All Harper could tell was that the woman was rather tall and wore her dark hair pulled back into a chignon. She carried a raincoat draped over one arm and a large handbag slung over her shoulder. Harper watched as the woman paused at the doorway to say something to the usher before appearing to hand him something. Harper turned her attention back to the audience and smiled.

"What happened to the young Muslim man?" a voice from the front row asked.

Harper considered the question for a moment before replying. "The UN observer managed to secure his release. This most likely occurred because there were several of us journalists on the scene bearing witness."

What she didn't reveal was that a week later the young Muslim was found shot to death beside the road along with six other men. She clicked the remote wand.

"Something lighter. 2016. Mardi Gras in Rio de Janeiro. One of my favorite celebration. So many wonderful and outrageous subjects," she said as a bejeweled, feathered and nearly nude coffee-colored woman filled the screen, her brilliant smile reflecting unbridled ecstasy.

And so it went for the rest of the evening, the photo exhibition followed by a short recitation of her background and a discussion of why she became a journalist, then followed by the obligatory questions and answers.

Fortunately, no one else asked the names of any more of her subjects or pressed her to comment too deeply on the circumstances that motivated her choice of subject matter. At the end, a handful of people lingered to purchase signed copies of one of her books. When the last of them had gone, her young host approached her and handed her a slip of paper.

"The woman," she said in explanation. "The one who asked about the soldier in the blue beret. She left you this."

Harper slipped on her glasses and read what was scrawled on the paper.

It's important that we talk. I would appreciate if you could meet me afterwards in the bar at the Slamic Hotel.

The note was unsigned. "Where is the Slamic Hotel?" she asked the young woman.

"It is not far. If you wish to go our driver will take you. Is there anything wrong?"

"No. I don't think so. Just an admirer," she said offering the woman a smile. "Tell your driver I just need to gather my things. Thank you so much for this opportunity. I enjoyed it."

She watched the young woman walk away and then studied the note again. What was this about, she wondered. What could this possibly have to do with Luke Marchand, someone she hadn't heard from or seen in… What? Twenty-four years? She fought back a sudden swirl of emotion, took a deep breath and then gathered up her laptop and coat and headed for the door.

2

The young woman was right about the Slamic Hotel being nearby, for it was no more than five minutes away by car. During the brief journey, the driver, an older gentleman who spoke only broken English, attempted to enlist Harper in a conversation about her earlier visit to the city, apparently having heard her anecdote back at the museum. He fumbled with his own narrative, regaling his role in the brief and victorious resistance effort the citizens of Slovenia undertook in facing down the Yugoslav Army. As he stopped in front of the hotel, he hurried to open her door and gave her an effusive embrace. Harper tipped him and told him not to wait.

A narrow side street fronted the hotel's unassuming entrance, the simple entryway opening into a street level anteroom that served as the hotel's bar. Harper paused in the lobby's threshold to survey the room and the handful of mostly empty tables. Two young couples sat at the bar along with an older woman with a greyhound stationed at her feet. It took Harper only a moment to make out the woman from the museum sitting alone at a table in the corner. The woman raised her hand in a tentative greeting as Harper made her way to the table.

They both eyed each other for a moment before Harper slipped out of her coat and dropped into the opposite chair. As a photographer, Harper prided herself on her ability to immediately observe every detail about a subject's appearance, no matter how minor. Therefore, it took her no more than a few seconds to capture the woman sitting across from her. Harper's first impression was that of a woman perhaps in her fifties. She had a delicate, fine-boned face, an olive complexion, and full lips. Only her crow's feet and the fine delta of wrinkles around her eyes hinted at her maturity. A combination of genetics and regular maintenance, Harper surmised. The eyes themselves were dark and oval. Her long black hair was pulled tightly from her face in a chignon that exposed her high forehead and a slight widow's peak.

"Would you like something to drink?" the woman asked, hoisting her wine glass. "I took the liberty of ordering you a gin martini. I'm sorry, but they don't have any Hendricks, only the local brands."

"Sure, The local stuff is fine."

The woman raised her hand to signal the bartender. "One never really knows a country until you drink their liquor. I was told this one is quite good. It is called Broken Bones."

Even though her English sounded polished, the cadence and her pronunciation gave her away. She was definitely German.

"You are wondering how I knew what you drink? I read the profile in the New Yorker. You are also partial to sushi and you get by on five hours of sleep."

Harper studied her for a moment. "Okay. So you think you know everything about me. So how about you tell me what the theatrics back at the museum were all about?"

"It brought you here, did it not?"

"If you want to keep me here though, you'll have to do more than buy me a drink. Who are you?"

The woman glanced up at the waiter who placed a martini at Harper's elbow. "*Hvala,*" she said to the waiter before looking back at Harper. "I doubt you ever knew my name. Luke wasn't exactly generous with details about his personal life. I am Adele, No? The name is still unfamiliar? Adele Marchand, The injured party," she added, with a smirk.

Harper looked at her in stunned silence, unsure how to respond. She was right. Lucretius Marchand hadn't been one to reveal many secrets. She took a sip of her martini. This Adele woman was right about the gin.

"That was a long time ago. And… Okay, I confess to knowing he was married. I won't make any excuses. It was just…"

Just what, she thought as she hesitated. For years, she ruminated about what an affair lasting all of two months really amounted to. What it had meant in the canvas of one's life. Obviously, not much since she never heard from Luke again after their brief, drug-fogged farewell on the tarmac at Aviano. The last image in her mind was of him leaning over her gurney, gripping her hand. He kissed her, or at least she remembered it that way, and then they wheeled her away,

"What would you like me to say? That it didn't mean anything? To either of us? It didn't. Or maybe I should just fall back on the old cliché that it was just the war. The way things were. I never knew your name," she added when Adele didn't say anything.

"I am disappointed," Adele said after a long moment. "You mean he never once uttered my name in the throes of a fuck," she said, with more amusement than resentment. "One of his other lovers confessed to me once that he did that all the time. Said my name in her bed." She flicked her eyes upwards before lowering her gaze and giving Harper a hard glance. "What do you make of that? I mean as a woman?"

Harper downed a healthy share of the martini, but held her silence.

"Don't worry," Adele said. "I don't bear you any ill will. Luke told me everything about you. Maybe more than I wanted to hear, but at some point…" Her words drifted away. "There comes a time when none of that really matters anyway. *Nicht war?*"

"You're still married?" Harper said, nodding at the diamond ring on Adele's finger.

"No," she replied after a moment's hesitation. "Luke and I were divorced two years ago. I still wear the ring though," she said, holding her hand up for Harper's inspection. "Perhaps, it is only my sentimental nature."

She downed the rest of her wine and raised the empty glass to the bartender. She looked back at Harper.

"Luke was unfaithful, as I was in my own way. Nevertheless, I still have feelings for him. I care for him much more than he probably deserves," she said with a shrug. "My mother used to tell me that you take what you can get out of life. Because sometimes that is all you will get."

"That sounds a lot like something my mama told me. Are you sure you didn't just plagiarize that from the New Yorker article?" Harper downed her martini and raised her glass to the bartender as he brought Adele's wine. "I'm sorry about you and Luke."

"As I said, I don't blame you. He was an easy man to be with. Probably too easy."

"And in his defense, he did have some integrity about certain things."

Adele smiled, but only her mouth moved. "*Ein bisschen war nie genug,*" she said quietly. "A little of him was never enough," she explained. "And more was too much. Something another of his lovers said to me when she was trying to come up with an excuse." She looked away as if lost in some thought.

"I understand what he saw in you," she said, turning back. "You seem to be a remarkable woman. No. I mean that. You are quite accomplished. Fearless, attractive. It must have been easy for him. You know, for him to fall for you."

"Fall for me? It was more he just stumbled into my bed. But you're wrong if you think it was easy for him."

Adele shrugged and waved her hand dismissively. "As I said, what is past is past. Let me ask you something. After I left the lecture, did you show any photos from your recent trip to Syria and Kurdistan?"

"No. Why do you ask?"

"I read the article you wrote for the Times. About what the camps were like. The interview you did with the leader of the PKK was wonderfully enlightening. Tell me, you seemed a bit vague as to whether you agree with your own government that they are terrorists. The Kurdistan Worker's Party."

Harper looked at her for a moment before replying. "Okay. You did your homework. Why the interest? "

Adele started to say something, and then started over. "Luke and I have a daughter. Magdalena. Maggie." Adele paused before going on. "She's adopted, just like your daughter. And she is…over there somewhere."

"What do you mean over there? In Kurdistan?"

"Syria. Perhaps Northern Iraq. I am not sure exactly where she is."

"I don't understand. What is she doing in Syria?"

Adele sighed and took a sip of her wine. "Maggie is a human rights lawyer in Munich. She went to the Syrian region of Kurdistan a few days before the invasion last month. She went with a man, her boyfriend Murat. He's Kurdish. Murat never would tell me exactly why he was going back, which didn't sit well with me. He said something about family commitments. Maggie wanted to see the refugee situation firsthand. She is involved in several refugee relief and resettlement programs. But the closer it got to her leaving, the more I was getting this…vibe from her that Murat was pressuring her to come along with him. I told her not to go. I begged her, actually. But in the end, she saw it as some kind of grand adventure."

"When did you last hear from her?"

"Three weeks ago. She called to tell me things were okay. Said they were in a safe place and not to worry. They were with Murat's family somewhere in northern Syria. Near a town called Qamishli. I am not sure if I am pronouncing it correctly."

"Al Qamishli. I know where it is. It's just across the border from Iraq. In the oil fields."

"Anyway, that was the last I heard from her. No emails. No Skype. Zoom. Nothing. I became worried. More than worried."

"Three weeks and no call? In a place like that" I can understand why you would be worried. It's not like she's on a beach holiday in Hawaii and is having too much fun to call."

Adele nodded in agreement. "So Luke went to find her."

"Luke went to Syria?"

"No. Iraq. There was no possibility of him getting into Syria. He has been there a week. He called when he arrived in Erbil. That is in Northern Iraq."

"I know where Erbil is."

"Yes, of course you do," she replied with a hint of sarcasm.. "So, I have not heard from him since. And he's not answering my calls or my emails. When he left Munich, we didn't exactly part on good terms. He had no idea of what Maggie was planning. He had been out of touch with both of us for a while. He does that. Last year, he bought a motorcycle. Since then…" She shrugged. "Every so often he calls me from Spain or Italy. He called once from Dubrovnik. I suspect he is not alone."

Harper arched her eyebrows but didn't say anything.

"When he found out what Maggie did, he became quite angry because I never told him, and even more so because I was unable to stop her. I could tell when he called from Erbil that he still had not forgiven me."

"So what exactly was he planning on doing? Did he even have any idea where she was?"

"No. After the invasion, there must have been many Syrian Kurdish refugees crossing into Iraq to get into the camps. All he said was he was going to start there. At the camps."

"I'm sure she made it to one of the Iraqi camps. Maybe he'll find her in one of them. But to be honest, it won't be easy. There could be several thousand or more people in any of them. Sometimes there's not even anyone in charge. It may take him a while to find her."

"Don't you understand? It's been a week. Luke would've called by now."

"I know what those camps are like. Getting word out isn't always easy. No cell, no WiFi, No..."

"*Du denkst ... !*" she said, loud enough to attract the attention of the people sitting at the bar. She paused and took a deep breath. "Do you really think no one would have a fucking SAT phone? Luke would have found a way to call me."

"I see what you mean."

"I have tried every back channel. Every contact."

"What kind of contacts?"

"I was in the *Bundeswehr*. The German Army. I was an intelligence analyst. It was how I met Luke. We were both stationed with NATO in Brussels. We married there. After we both retired, we moved to Germany. I started to do some free lance consulting. Corporate research. Vetting potential employees, mostly. And sometimes it requires me to research competitors," she added with a hint of a smile. "Therefore, I still have many contacts from the old life. Foreign Ministry people. The intelligence community," she added. "When Luke didn't get in touch, I started calling in favors to see if anyone could help or knew anything."

"Look, Adele. My advice is to sit tight and wait. Something will turn up."

"I cannot do that. I need to know where they are, and that they are both safe. I was hoping..." She turned away, then shook her head and looked at Harper. "I was hoping that maybe you would come with me and use your contacts to help me find them."

Harper shook her head in disbelief. "Come with you? To Syria? In the first place, you're crazy to want to go there. Second, what you're asking... It may not be doable. You know as well as I do that the Turkish military and the Syrians aren't letting any Western journalists near there. I doubt ether of them are in any great hurry to have the world see what's going on there."

"It is doable. Enough money changes hands, and borders become amazingly porous."

"And I can speak from experience. Just because a border appears amazingly porous doesn't mean crossing isn't dangerous. Have you contacted your Foreign Ministry? Or the State Department? She's a US citizen, isn't she?"

"She has dual citizenship. She uses her German passport to travel. It is a little safer. And yes, I notified them both. They both said they would look into it. You know what that probably means."

"And what about all these so called contacts? They should be plugged in enough in that part of the world to provide you with the names of someone there who might help."

"That isn't an option right now. Besides, this is a personal matter."

"Like I said, maybe you should wait it out a while longer."

Harper could see the disappointment blossom on Adele's face. "Very well. I plan on going regardless."

Harper shook her head in annoyance. "Okay. Look, getting to Erbil may not be very difficult. But once you leave the city you'll have to deal with the Peshmerga, the Kurdish Army. Once you leave Kurdish territory, then you've got militias of every fucking stripe. Plus there're always the usual bandits and *hajji* wannabes. The closer you get to the Syrian border you'll probably also deal with the Iraqi Army and the various Shia militias. There'll be checkpoints every twenty miles. If she's still in Syria, it will even be more difficult."

Adele didn't say anything.

"You're thinking I owe you. Is that it? I owe you for something that happened twenty-four years ago."

"You owe Luke. He saved your life, did he not?" she said, her voice betraying a hint of anger.

"Owe? He…" She resisted revealing what she had long repressed. Those debts were long cancelled and forgotten. Or were they? Harper paused as the bartender placed her martini before her, her gaze never leaving Adele's. "Yes, he did. But…I can't go. I promised my daughter, my agent, all my friends, my goddamn therapist. I promised them all that I wouldn't go into any more conflict zones. I'm sixty years old for chrissakes. I've paid my dues."

"I realize that. The risks you have taken. I saw that in your photos. And yet, you have never let that stop you. A normal person would have…"

"Yeah, well. I'm not normal," she said, cutting her off. "Just ask my shrink. She had me down after three sessions as one of those people who think there's never going to be enough. Enough interviews. Enough risks. Enough awards." Enough men, she could have easily added. "The obsession to take one more photograph. The one that might make someone care. And then one day I realized that what I didn't have enough of was time. Breast cancer can do that. That and having a daughter. You must have heard of Marie Colvin? She used to say there were old war correspondents, and bold ones, but very few ones that were bold and still tempting fate at a ripe old age."

She thought again of that night huddled in the basement in Aleppo, she and Marie sharing Kentucky bourbon from a canteen and trading stories. Did Marie have any premonition of her death? She must have, but it didn't stop her. She looked back at Adele.

"I imagine Luke told you about what happened in Sarajevo. Then you should understand."

She took another swallow of the martini and began the mental inventory. It was something she had promised her agent she would do whenever she was tempted to travel somewhere too far off the grid. She would list the places in her mind, reciting them like some kind of validating mantra. Sarajevo was only the beginning. There was the Sudan and the panic she felt as the *mujahedeen* surrounded her and Sonny. The suffocating terror she experienced hanging by her wrists from a rafter in that dank cellar in Honduras. Syria and the artillery shelling of Homs. Her brief captivity by the Syrian Army. The numbing cold of the mountains. Beirut and having to bear witness to the assassination of the Syrian dissident as he sat across the table from her. Sierra Leone and the unremitting reek of death. The pervasive awareness of the Ebola and its lethal randomness. Her abduction in the Liberian jungle. That bloody afternoon in Guatemala City. She could go on and on.

"I can't," she said, meeting Adele's eyes. "I've lost something. The need... the desire to live like that. I've lost my courage, maybe." Or my death wish, she thought. "I can't."

Adele nodded and fell silent for a moment. "I have to confess that I came here tonight partly out of curiosity. But when I saw the photo of your daughter, I realized you would probably sacrifice everything for her. Yes? So you must understand what I would do to find Maggie. So perhaps I am calling in debts wherever I can find them. And I am also doing something I am not very good at, and that is asking for help."

"And I'm telling you there were times in the past when you could've asked me, and I would've gone with you in a New York minute. And it wouldn't be out of any sense of obligation or misplaced altruism, but just because there would be a story. If that sounds callous and self-serving, you'd be right."

"Fair enough. All I really need are any contacts you might have in Kurdistan."

"The reality is you're going to need more than that. You'll need a translator. A driver you can trust. And once you get off the beaten path you'll want a couple of bodyguards. And even then, it might be hard just getting to some of those camps. And then what? You're going to stroll through them showing everyone Maggie's picture? I know I'm sounding pessimistic. I just want you to know what you're getting into."

"I am not unaccustomed... a virgin to this kind of thing. I served a tour in Afghanistan. I will manage."

Harper sighed and thought for a moment. "I tell you what I can do. I'll try to reach out to some people in Erbil. Maybe they know somebody that can help. Arrange for drivers and such. It's always a friend of a friend who might know somebody. None of which is ever reassuring."

"She is my daughter. I have to do this."

"Okay, I fly back to New York tomorrow. I'll ask around. I might even be able to get you press credentials."

"Press credentials would be helpful. I must tell you though that there isn't much time. If something happened, I mean. I must find them."

"I'll do what I can. I promise."

Adele dug into her purse and retrieved a pen and a piece of paper. "Here is my email and cell number," she said, jotting down the information. She pushed it across the table and rose to her feet. "Thank you for your time," she said rather brusquely and started to walk off.

Harper grabbed her arm. "I'm sorry. About Sarajevo. About Luke. About everything."

Adele gently pulled her arm free and walked out of the bar. Harper finished her martini and waved to the bartender. Why not, she thought. Maybe it would help her to sleep, although she knew better. Tonight, she'd be sharing a bed with memories of Sarajevo.

3

SARAJEVO, BOSNIA
OCTOBER, 1995

"Major Marchand, I do believe you've made me see stars," Harper said, lifting her head from the coarse folded blanket that served as a pillow to gaze out the window. The night sky erupted with a sudden luminescence that lent a ghostly glow to the low ceiling of grey clouds. She watched for a few seconds as the nimbus of light from the parachute flare drifted from view, leaving them again in darkness. She rolled onto her stomach and stretched like a cat, head down, rump up.

"I could make a call and arrange for a few more flares. Or we could try for the stars again," Luke said, probing the blanket between them for the ashtray.

"Are you sure it's okay to leave the curtains open?"

"Sure. You know as well as I do that the Bosnians cleared out most of the snipers a few weeks ago. And with this cloud cover, any spotters still in those hills are blind. Don't forget we're on the safe side of the building."

She heard the scratch of a match, and a second later saw his face in the flare of yellow light as he relit his cigar, the angles of his brows and cheekbones drawn more boldly by the wavering light. He tossed her the book of matches before blowing out the match.

"Put this in your scrapbook. The Holiday Inn Sarajevo. Your Home Away From Home. When your home's been bombed to shit," he added without sarcasm.

Harper picked up the match book, rose from the bed and walked over to the window. Another parachute flare suddenly illuminated the expanse of dark rooftops that sloped up the hills to the north of the city. The light exposed a small concentric web of shattered glass where the window had been struck by an errant bullet. She pressed her hand against the dime-sized hole in its center and felt the cold air seeping through her fingers.

"I wish I didn't have to go," she said.

She heard him get up from the bed, and a moment later, felt him press himself against her back, his arms encircling her waist.

"I don't see where you have much choice. Your mother needs you," he said, as his hands slid down her belly and grazed her pubis. She reached up with her one hand and stroked his face.

Two days ago, she had received word that her mother had suffered another series of mild strokes. Luke had arranged for her to fly out this very night on a Spanish Air Force relief flight headed for Aviano, the US Air Force base in Italy. Tonight had started with a farewell alfresco meal of canned tuna, three day old bread, a tired bunch of grapes and bottle of Algerian wine, followed by a long and languorous session of lovemaking.

"Your mother isn't the only reason you need to go. You've over-stayed your time here, and you know it. Two tours here are plenty."

"Three," she said. "You forget I came here in '91 when this shitty little war was just starting."

"Even more reason. I see that look on your face when you lower the camera."

"Yeah? Well…" She really had no reply. "So you'll still be here when I get back?"

"Leave, Harper. And don't come back," he added, gripping her tighter.

27

She wriggled free from his embrace and turned to look at him. For a brief instant, she could see his face in the reflected light of the flare before it drifted out of sight, leaving them in darkness again.

"You don't want me to come back, do you? Is it because your wife may show up here one of these days? You said she might pull some strings and fly in for the weekend. If that's your only reason, I understand."

When he didn't say anything, she walked over to the dresser and started to slip on her bra and panties. He stood there staring out the window for a moment before he raised his wrist to his face to check the luminous dial of his watch.

"You're going have to leave in another forty-five minutes to make it to the airport on time. I bribed those Spaniards pilots with a case of bourbon but that doesn't mean they'll wait forever." He turned and looked at her. "Even though part of me wishes you'd miss the flight."

"Oh, yeah? Which part is that?" she asked with more sarcasm than she intended.

"Come on, Harper. You know it's more than just… "

"A fuck? Just one of your overseas tour bonuses?"

"Harper. Don't. "

"Look, I get it. You're married to… What's her name? You've never said."

"It's not…"

"You don't have to remind me that we both went into this with eyes wide open," she said, wriggling into her jeans. "It's been great. I don't know if I could've survived the past couple of months without you, but let's not make it more than what it is. Okay?"

He reached for her arm but she pulled away.

"Don't, Luke. We need to just leave it."

"Why are you suddenly so… catty about this?" He started to say something more but the buzzing of his SAT phone stopped him. He picked it up from the dresser and disappeared into the bathroom. She started to stuff clothes into her duffle bag before hurling it against the wall.

"Shit."

Why was this so hard? Why couldn't she just tell him? She had half-convinced herself that this was nothing more than a casual fling, the kind of thing that happens when you grasp at any semblance of heat in a cold world. Living the way she did, chronicling mankind's worst, that and her growing cynicism all made easy to confuse love with desire. She should've learned a lesson from her train wreck of a marriage, all thirteen months of it. It seemed to always boil down to the question of how something that felt this good invariably end so shabbily? It only made it worse that the possibility they might never see each other again had now been broached.

It made her think of something her mother had once told her. "Baby, if you're gonna be with a man, better be prepared to bleed. And not just the first time."

"Oh, Mama," she muttered as she picked up the duffel bag from the floor and began again to pack her few belongings. She looked up and saw Luke standing in the bathroom doorway watching her.

"I have to go," he said. "Something's going on over in Vogosca. Maybe some Serb infiltrators or maybe somebody's just nervous and shooting at shadows." He picked up his flak jacket and helmet from the floor. "Don't forget the APC is going to pick you up downstairs at ten."

When Harper didn't say anything, he walked over and took her in his arms. He tried to kiss her but she turned her face away.

"I could say a lot of different things," he said. "Things that might sound good. And some of them would be things I really mean."

She couldn't tell if he was joking or not. "Are you sure that came out right? It sounds like you've had plenty of practice muddying the water."

"Come on, Harper. Let's not do this. What do you want? You want me to say you mean more to me than anyone else I've ever been with? That I'll leave my wife? Is that what you need to hear?"

"No. Maybe I just want you to hurt a little. That's all."

"Well then mission fucking accomplished. Okay?" he said with surprising bitterness. "Don't miss the bus," he said and started for the door. He stopped and turned to face her. "I wish things were different. I do. It's just the way thing are."

Dammit! Tell him.

He blew her a kiss and walked out, closing the door quietly behind him.

It took every ounce of willpower to not open the door and shout his name. She stood there for a long moment, her breath shallow and rapid. After a minute, she stuffed the last of her clothes in the bag and went over to the window. Somewhere up in the hills a fire blazed. She pressed her forehead against the cold glass only to pull back in alarm at the rattle of gunfire, this time closer. Maybe Luke was right. It was time to go.

4

Harper strolled across the dark hotel lobby to peer once more out the two shattered windows that framed the boarded up front entranceway. She could just make out where someone had spray painted the words 'PAZI SNAJPER' in red on a sheet of plywood that sat propped against a fire hydrant. Beware Sniper. Since the beginning of the siege three years ago, it had been foolhardy to use the front entrance due to the Serbian snipers and artillery in the hills across the river. For that same reason, the rooms in the front of the hotel remained vacant. Any guests making their way to their room were required to use the side entrance, and once disembarking from the main elevator, walk counterclockwise to their rooms in the rear to avoid exposing themselves.

She turned and walked back across the deserted lobby, its only occupant the elderly desk manager who seemed engrossed in a newspaper he read by the light of a small lantern. The two security guards who usually dozed on one of the lobby's grimy sofas were nowhere to be seen. She made her way through the maze of mismatched chairs to the side entrance where Rodavan leaned against the fender of his Skoda smoking a cigarette. He had come for a final goodbye and to give Harper a pair of mittens his wife Nadia had knitted as a farewell gift.

It had rained earlier, and the air, rather than being cleansed, smelled of diesel exhaust, the muddy river and moldy rubble. Harper stood there a moment and stared up into the light mist drifting down in the anemic light of the lone street lamp.

"Your major is late," Rodavan said, tapping his wrist watch.

"I told you. He's not coming. He's sending an APC. Let me have one of your cigarettes," she said.

"I thought you said no more." He reached into the pocket of his jacket and retrieved a crumpled pack of Marlboros.

"I hope that isn't the last of the packs I gave you," she said, deftly removing a cigarette. She waited as he fumbled for his lighter. "Before I forget," she said, leaning into the flame as he cupped his hands against the drizzle. She reached into her pocket and pulled out a roll of currency and stuffed it into the pocket of his jacket.

"What is this?" he asked.

"I won't need any money until I get to New York. Use it for petrol and food for the kids. Maybe buy Nadia something nice. Just don't spend it all on black market cigarettes."

Soon after Harper arrived in Sarajevo, a fellow journalist recommended she hire Rodavan to be her driver and translator. He had become more than that; confidante, companion, and protector. On more than one occasion, she had shared a meal with his wife and children. Before the war, he had studied to become a dentist. Now, he shepherded journalists from one mishap to the next in a dented Skoda he had inherited from a friend who had fled to Croatia.

Rodavan placed one hand over his heart and nodded. "*Hvala prijatelju.* You are most kind. How can I ever repay you?"

She sucked the cigarette smoke deep into her lungs and exhaled. "It is you I must repay, my friend," she replied, affectionately placing her hand on his shoulder.

In the distance she could again hear the rattle of gunfire and what might have been an explosion. The rain and the surrounding buildings made it difficult to tell where it was coming from. Maybe Vogosca. She thought of Luke and hoped he was safe.

Rodavan squinted at his watch again. "If you do not leave soon it will be too late. Perhaps, I should drive you. One last time, yes?"

"Do you think it's safe?"

Rodavan shrugged. "I think no snipers tonight. There have been no incidents on the road to the airport in many weeks now. The UN patrols, yes? It should be okay."

Harper thought about it for a moment, and then took a final drag of the cigarette and nodded. "Okay, let's go then."

Rodavan flicked his cigarette into the street and pulled a chamois skin from the pocket of his jeans. The Skoda's windshield wipers no longer worked, so he wiped the windshield the best he could, making sure the word PRESS was visible where he had painted it across the top in large white letters.

Harper forced open the badly dented passenger side door and tossed her duffle into the back seat and climbed in. The car smelled of damp upholstery and cigarette smoke, an odor that she found strangely comforting. Rodavan pulled slowly out onto the deserted street in front of the hotel. The boulevard, Zmaja od Bosne, was named after a local folk hero referred to as the Dragon of Bosnia, At the height of the siege, the street had been referred to as Sniper's Alley. Cars and pedestrians ventured across its intersections at their peril.

Ever cautious, Rodavan was careful to use only his parking lights in order to avoid drawing any unwarranted attention. At this time of night, the street was deserted, mostly by self-imposed curfew. After a minute or so, they came upon a UN roadblock manned by a half-dozen blue helmeted soldiers huddled around a white armored personnel carrier. Rodavan slowed, but then was waved through once the soldiers noticed the word PRESS painted on the windshield.

He lighted another cigarette, leaning into the flame, highlighting the contours of his angular face. She regarded him silently, fixing his face into her memory. He had a nervous, intense face, and spoke out of one side of his mouth, a smoker's habit. He seemed to only smile when faced with unpleasantness; an interrogation at a roadblock, the wail of a grieving widow. But he seemed to never show fear of any sort.

"Nadia will worry, won't she? About you being out this late?"

He lifted his shoulders in an eloquent shrug and cocked his head in reply.

"I must remember when I get to New York to print the photos I took when we had that little picnic in the park. The one with Nadia and the kids on the swing. And you washing this car. I'll find a way to send them to you. Maybe one of my journalist friends can drop them off."

"You will not return?"

"I don't know. It depends." She fell silent for a moment before going on. "I want to ask you something. Why is it you never seem afraid? All this time, you've never showed the slightest fear. Even that time those Serbian soldiers stopped our car."

"It is the war. What can one do? If it is one's time, then…" he concluded through a mouthful of smoke. "There is a Muslim saying. A proverb, yes? When the Angel of Death approaches it is terrible. When he reaches you, it is bliss."

"Jesus, I'll have to remember that one. I'm sure it'll come in handy some day."

"You must also remember that this war… the siege, will not last forever. I must believe that. Otherwise…" His words drifted off as he slowed as they passed the charred skeleton of a bus cantilevered over a ditch on the edge of the roadway. The wreckage, a leftover from when the narrow corridor leading from the city proper to the airport was often a life or death undertaking, Most of the terrain on either side of the corridor had been cleared of trees as a security measure, but here and there still stood clumps of stunted pine that were now cloaked in patches of thick fog.

The road, an uneven quilt of muddy turf and potholed asphalt, required a cautious pace that in those earlier times made for treacherous driving even under the best of circumstances. As they rounded the last curve before the checkpoint, they could just make out its lights through the murky mist. Rodavan slowed and blinked his high beams so as to not surprise some trigger happy sentry.

They crept slowly forward, finally coming to a halt some twenty or so yards before the gate shack beside the metal barrier that blocked the road. A troop carrier with Bosnian Army markings sat parked beside the shack. Rodavan slipped the Skoda into neutral and pulled out his pack of cigarettes. He fumbled to remove the last of his cigarettes, all the while not taking his eyes off the gate shack. No one was visible inside its brightly lit interior.

"If there're Bosnians on duty, they're probably asleep. Or drunk," Harper said, craning her head to look around.

Rodavan started to light his cigarette, but paused, the unlit lighter halfway to his mouth, his gaze fixed on the seemingly empty gate shack.

"Where do you think they are?" Harper asked.

He grunted, and then lowered his lighter and leaned forward over the steering wheel.

"What? Do you see something?"

He stared a couple of seconds more, and then reached for the gear shift. "We must go," he whispered. He slipped the Skoda into reverse and started to slowly back up. In that same instant, Harper saw them. Three figures dressed in camouflage quickly emerged from the brush beside the gate shack, their rifles pointed at the Skoda.

Rodavan shoved Harper down onto the seat and mashed his foot down on the accelerator. The car rocketed backward, weaving wildly back down the roadway behind them. It all happened so quickly - the sound of rifle fire, the windshield shattering, Rodavan yelling, the car spinning out of control, and then only the tinny wailing of the car horn, She lifted her head. In the dim light of the dashboard lights all she could see was Rodavan slumped over the wheel.

35

"Rodavan! Rodavan!"

She tugged at him, her hand touching something wet and hot. He fell towards her, and she heard him make a gurgling, choking sound. She must've screamed then for she could hear nothing else; nothing until the yelling of someone, and the sound of the passenger side door being wrenched open.

Someone yanked her by the collar of her jacket, dragging her out of the car and tossing her onto the muddy roadway. A boot came down on her back. She twisted onto her side, her arm shielding her face. She could see them more clearly now in the Skoda's headlights. Camouflage fatigues, black ski masks. Three of them. Maybe more. Someone kicked her in the side.

"Press! Journalist! *Novinar!*" she yelled as she gasped for air.

One of them laughed, another commented something unintelligible, and then she felt herself being dragged through the mud towards the gate shack. One of them kicked open the door as another flung her onto the floor. The sudden bright light disoriented her. She lifted her head and saw the two bloodied bodies of the Bosnian guards heaped into the corner.

"*Novinar.* Journalist. Do you understand? Please!"

One of them twisted her onto her back, and struck her in the face with his fist. She felt her lip split and tasted the blood in her mouth. He sat on top of her and then lifted up his ski mask and smiled. He looked young, no more than an adolescent.

"Please."

He struck her again, this time harder on the side of her head and she felt something crack in her cheekbone. She thought she heard he and the others laughing, and then someone stepped on her thigh. The one on top of her rose on his knees and turned her onto her stomach. She felt something cut into the back of her jeans, felt them being jerked down.

"No! Please! Don't. *Molimo vas!*"

And then someone struck her on the side of the head, and then there was nothing.

"Harper. Oh, God. Harper. Can you hear me?"

The voice seemed to come from a long distance away. Someone was trying to lift her head up. She winced in pain. It seemed her face was stuck tight against the cold concrete. She opened her eyes, but everything was blurred.

"It's Luke, baby. Don't move. Help's on the way."

And then nothing.

5

EMMA WILLARD SCHOOL FOR GIRLS
TROY, NEW YORK
NOVEMBER 20TH, 2019

Harper had always found the parents' lounge quite comfortable and inviting; plush Oriental carpets atop dark oak flooring, Venetian plastered walls in a soothing taupe, a blazing fireplace, and a large picture window with a view of the Hudson River. All would be complete if it only had an open bar, she thought as she lifted her feet onto the refrigerator-sized leather Ottoman. She would settle for a mini-bar, on the honor system, of course, but she doubted the tight-assed matron in reception would let her run a tab.

Alcohol was the last thing she needed right now. What she really wanted was her own bed and ten hours of dreamless, Ambien-fueled sleep. She couldn't recall the last time she had slept for more than an hour or two at a time. Not her last night in Ljubljana, and surely not in the terminal at Charles De Gaulle awaiting the flight to Newark. The overseas flight itself remained a fog of half-eaten meals, two glasses of wine, several cups of coffee, and a glimpse of a mindless movie, all interspersed with perhaps an hour nap. Then there was the short layover in Newark before the flight to Albany.

She suspected the car rental agent thought she was intoxicated, but it was merely her exhaustion and the melancholia brought on by the memories the talk in Ljubljana had elicited. The lecture had only set the stage. Enter

Adele, the main act, turning over the soil and dredging up traumas that were never completely below the waterline of her psyche. Her therapist made sure she never forgot them. Face it. You'll never be without them, she had admonished Harper. You just have to learn to deal with them differently. The therapist's dictum was to not dwell on the past, but to live in the present, and to be surprised by the future. If it were only that simple.

Adele's petition for help had consumed Harper's every waking moment. Her consequent agitation stemmed more from a nagging sense of obligation than anything else. She could argue that the burden of this obligation was misplaced, and that any involvement on her part would prove misguided. Somehow, that argument held less and less water as her fixation grew. In the end, she would do what she could, but there was no way she was going to Kurdistan, mostly because of the lanky figure now striding through the doorway.

"*Mi Mama*," Funaya shouted, using the Krio endearment she had used from the moment Harper had rescued her from the orphanage in Freetown.

Harper struggled to her feet, bleary and stiff from travel. Before she could fully stand, Funaya embraced her with sufficient eagerness to make them both tumble back onto the sofa.

"Baby, baby. I am so happy to see you," Harper said, cradling Funaya's head to her chest. In the past, this had proven to be the go-to response whenever Funaya required comfort and confirmation. She held her like this for a long moment, taking in the scent of her coarse hair; shampoo and cinnamon oil. "Let me look at you," Harper said, holding her at arm's length. "Do they ever feed you here? For what I'm paying, I expect at least a little accumulation of body fat."

Funaya laughed. "Mama, I eat like a pig. You said you liked me like this."

"I do." She hugged her again. Decent nutrition had indeed allowed Funaya to blossom. At seventeen, she had the graceful, well-honed physique of a gazelle – lean, lithe and devoid of the awkwardness of pubescence. She was a beautiful young woman with fine features, a dark chocolate complexion and eyes older than her face.

It had been five years since she brought Funaya back with her to New York from Sierra Leone. For the first year, Harper had refused any assignments, committing all of her time and energy into caring for the then scrawny, fearful orphan. Harper home schooled her, not only in the basics, but had also instilled in her the nuance and customs of the ways of the world. She exposed her to everything – arts and culture, both classic and popular, American sports and food, along with the joys and the dangers of a world that must have seemed to her bewildering and foreign.

To Harper's astonishment, Funaya had proven to possess a graceful resilience and an inherent intelligence that allowed her to quickly integrate into every setting to which she was exposed. She had studied at the Willard School for over a year now, and even her teachers were amazed at her progress and abilities.

"So how's school?"

Funaya shrugged. "It is difficult. I don't enjoy math. I am unable to see the point."

"You'll get no argument there. You still like the art class and English though?"

"Very much. And French. *J'aime le françai.*"

"*Bien.,* And friends?"

"A challenge, yes? I have two very close friends. One of them is an orphan, too. From Uganda. The other girls…" She shrugged.

"You don't have to tell me about girls. I've been there."

"Yes, but I made a mistake. I told a girl about my mother. My first mother. And how she died. It seems that in a matter of days, the other girls knew. I could see it in their eyes. It was very much like it was in Sierra Leone. The fear. As if my backpack and books had Ebola on them. It is like I am a pariah. That is a new word I learned."

"It'll pass. At least with the ones that matter. When you come home for the holidays, I'll give you a tutorial in dealing with the members of our own sex. And boys?"

"What boys? There are no boys here."

"But you talk about them. Dream about them, I bet."

Funaya smiled. "I like it when we talk of boys instead of sisterhood."

"So I'll pick you up on the 19th, right?"

Funaya studied her. "What are you not telling me?"

Harper shook her head, partly in denial, partly in amazement. Funaya possessed an uncanny ability to read her every thought. A year spent continuously in each other's company along with some innate clairvoyance rendered Harper an open book to Funaya's observations.

"Where are you going now?" she asked.

"I'm not going anywhere."

"Bullshit. Another new word I learned. I like that word very much. It's useful. Don't try to bullshit me. Yes? That is correct usage? Come on. I can see you are already gone. In your head."

"I'm just tired. But…" There was no use. They had few secrets. "Something came up in Slovenia. Someone asked for my help. Help I can't give. The strange thing is this woman wants me to help her find her daughter. Her daughter is also adopted."

Funaya arched her eyebrows. "Then you must help her find this daughter. It is only right that you do this."

"It's not that simple. I would have to go somewhere far away and possibly dangerous. I told you I wasn't going to do that anymore."

"No matter. I trust you," she replied, putting her arms around Harper's neck.

Harper laughed. "Why do I feel like you're the mother?"

"You told me just three weeks ago that I possessed wisdom far beyond my years, did you not?"

"That must've been after a couple of martinis. Look, I'm going to try to help this woman, but without going somewhere. Okay? Listen, I have to go. I'm tired, and you've got volleyball practice. I'll call this weekend so we can make some plans for the holidays. Dinner reservations somewhere nice, maybe a play or two, then go to Manhattan and ogle the boys."

"Ogle? What does that mean?"

"To undress them with our eyes."

"I believe I am the only girl here with a shameless mother."

They hugged and kissed, After Funaya left the lounge, Harper called and made a reservation at a hotel she usually stayed at while visiting the school. Her flight back didn't leave until 10 AM, enough time for eight or nine hours of sleep. She sat there a minute ruminating before dialing another number. He answered on the first ring.

"*Hola, chica.* How was the City of Dragons?" Manny asked, referring to Ljubljana.

"Dangerous."

"I won't ask. So what can I do for you?"

Manny Obregon was Harper's researcher extraordinaire. She had used his services to not only plan trips, but to seek out contacts, obtain little known information and gossip, and provide the sort of in depth background material only someone like him could provide.

"I need some information. Ready?" She waited as Manny found something to write with. "Adele Marchand. Lives in Munich, Ex-military. Their army, not ours. Ex-husband Lucretius Marchand. Goes by Luke." She spelled out Lucretius.

"He's retired from our army. Their daughter, Magdalena. A human rights lawyer in Munich. Then, everything you can find out about the current situation on the ground in Kurdistan. Up to date maps of who controls

42

what, the security situation, getting around. The usual stuff. And look to see what you can find out about any of the refugee camps on either side of the Iraqi border. One more thing, see if you still have a current email address for that journalist, Ras al-Saumar. The guy we used to arrange that driver for me the last time."

"How soon do you need this?"

"I'll be home after lunch tomorrow."

"You're paying overtime, right? I mean we're talking an all nighter here. You want me to get you a plane ticket, too?"

"Not yet. But if you run out of things to do, you can look at flights into Erbil."

"I'm on it. Meet you at Devoción for coffee?" he asked, referring to their regular coffee shop.

"Sure. Let me know when you'll be there," she replied and hung up. She sat there a moment longer balancing in her mind her reticence and that nagging sense of obligation. Funaya was right. If she at least didn't make the effort to help Adele, she would never let herself off the hook. She pushed herself to her feet, groaning at her stiff joints, and walked out of the lounge to her rental car.

6

The entryway of the Devoción coffee house in Williamsburg looked more like the portal of an upscale office building with its sleek steel and glass doors and its airy, two story sky-lit atrium interior. One entire wall consisted of a vertical garden of tropical plants and small coffee trees. At mid-afternoon, it sat relatively empty, the after lunch crowd fully- caffeinated and back in their squirrel cages. Harper ordered a large Americano and settled into a corner table to wait for Obregon.

Manny Obregon was a Puerto Rican of African heritage with a café au lait complexion and an Afro twice the size of his already enormous head. His stature was no less intimidating. At six foot six and nearly three hundred pounds, he was the first person one might notice in any crowd. He was an ex-con that Harper had cultivated some years ago at a cocktail party. He had served three years with time off for good behavior after being handed five to seven for computer hacking the Bank of America. Fortunately, the prosecuting attorney had never discovered that Manny had also hacked several government agencies, most notably the Department of Defense personnel files. Since his release, Manny settled into the straight and narrow, sticking to research and simple vetting.

At three PM sharp, Manny shambled through the doors, ordered his usual, a double Macchiato, and joined Harper. After carefully setting down his cup, he placed an open satchel containing a laptop and what appeared to be thick sheaf of papers in the middle of the table before easing his bulk into the chair opposite Harper.

"You know you're a lot of work, *chica*," he purred in his lilting Puerto Rican accent.

"So I've been told. How are you?"

"Thank you for finally asking. My sugar is under control," he said, referring to his diabetes. "And your last job paid for two gold crowns," he said, opening wide and tapping a gold molar. He had the kind of fleshy, voluptuous mouth that kept one from noticing his rather small eyes which were hidden behind thick, Coke bottle lenses. "Mia is well also, but she may have contracted my sugar."

Mia was his morbidly obese Maine Coon. Harper had seen the cat once, on the sole occasion she had ever set foot in Manny's apartment. His domicile more than met her expectations, for it was crammed with what appeared at first glance to be poorly organized bookshelves, waist-high stacks of magazines and newspapers, and three desks holding enough computer hardware to stock a wall of shelves at Best Buy. His uncluttered, modern and well-equipped kitchen was his only nod to good housekeeping.

"Forgive me for asking, but what are you up to this time?" he asked, slurping his macchiato. "I mean, why the interest in Kurdistan? You were just there."

Harper shrugged noncommittally. "I need some current background for an article for The Economist."

"And these Marchand people? I have to tell you that the three of them are quite interesting. I will infer something here. *El soldado,* this Luke Marchand. Let me guess. You knew him in Bosnia, right? You were both there at the same time. I checked the dates."

"Ah, that's why I pay you so handsomely. Never mind. Cut to the chase."

Manny took a long drink of his coffee, wiped his lips with the back of his hand, and removed the thick manila binder from the satchel.

"I emailed you an attachment with all of this, but I know how much you like hard copy." He dumped the binder in front of her. "I'll just give you the big picture because unfortunately that is all I could come up with on short notice. If you want more, I can put in more time."

"Just tell me what you have."

"Lucretius Marchand. Lucretius is such an imposing name. The Roman poet, yes? Anyway, a retired colonel of infantry. Born in Kansas, educated at West Point. He had a relatively illustrious career. Made his bones so to speak in the First Gulf War leading a forward infantry battalion. Then did a tour as an instructor at the Army's War College. A stint with NATO in Brussels. UN observer in Bosnia. Then a Pentagon assignment followed by Afghanistan in 2002. Baghdad in 2003. He seemed to be climbing the ladder. He made full colonel age 47. Then in 2008, two years short of thirty years, he resigned his commission. In my experience, that raises a red flag. Maybe he was forced out. I can put you in touch with someone who might be able to dig deeper."

"Go on."

Manny took another swallow of coffee before going on. "After he retired, he moved to West Germany. *El es muy mysterioso.* An enigma, yes? Not one who is revealed by a simple Google search. I had to check a ton of websites. He has a small apartment outside of Munich. He's not a joiner of anything. Not so much as a gym membership. There is no proof of any employment. He has an email addresses he rarely uses. He has one bank account, a registration for a BMW motorcycle and a car. Other than a recent flight to Baghdad, he doesn't travel much. At least outside of the Euro Zone. If you're wondering how I know he hasn't left the Euro Zone in three years is because I discovered a back door into the EU Immigration Agency. Don't look at me like that. I'm behaving. Mostly."

"Did you find any recent photos?"

"Not really anything current. Now, this ex-wife is more interesting," he said, leafing through the file. "Adele Krause Marchand. I looked up what

Krause meant in English. Frizzy. Isn't that weird? Your last name means frizzy. Anyway, both of her parents were killed in a car accident when she was just eight, leaving her as an only child without relatives. She spent the next nine years in Germany's foster care system. Somebody must've put in the work with her though because she received a full scholarship to the University of Heidelberg. Majored in Russian studies. Afterwards, she joined the Army, theirs, not ours. The *Bundeswehr*. I love saying that word. *Bundeswehr*."

"They recruited her as an intelligence analyst. She's had assignments at the German Ministry of Defense, attended our Army's staff college in Fort Leavenworth, Kansas. She spent a couple of years at NATO Headquarters in Brussels. The only action she ever saw was a six month tour in Afghanistan attached to some Kraut special ops outfit. She did several Eastern European tours as a military attaché or embassy staff. One of these tours was in Ukraine in 1995. Seems that's where she adopted Magdalena. She retired several years after Luke did. They must've had one of those marriages with a lot of time spent apart. Can you imagine? Married and two different armies. They were living in Munich and divorced two years ago. No surprise there."

"After she retired, she became a consultant. Her website advertises corporate security, background checks, research, which may be an offhand way of saying industrial espionage. A lot of the same stuff I do, only with a decent salary and health insurance. I was only able to run down the name of her only current client. Armstrong Technics. It's headquartered in DC. It provides surveillance and cyber warfare equipment to the military. She doesn't leave a lot of footprints so to speak, but…. Are you ready? This is what you pay me the big bucks for. I found one interesting little detail. Her name is listed under the Trade Section at the German Embassy in Prague."

"It's funny she didn't mention that," Harper mumbled. "Trade Section?"

Manny shrugged. "The embassy site says the section is involved in economic research and fostering trade between their two countries. If you read spy novels you know that's the department where they always hide the spies. Don't worry. I don't plan on digging around in that hole. She does make frequent trips to Bonn. And two trips to Washington D.C. in the past year. And of course, frequent trips to Munich where she has an apartment. Those are the broad strokes. The minor details you can read for yourself."

"And the daughter?"

""Born in Ukraine 1994. Adele found her in an orphanage in '95. Brought her back to Germany and later stateside."

"When in '95 did she adopt her?"

Manny checked his notes. "Looks like October. ¿Por qué?" He gave her the kind of look that telegraphed both discretion and inquisitiveness. It was one of the things that drew her to his personality.

"Never mind. Go on."

"She graduated cum laude at twenty at UMass, then law school at Georgetown. After graduating from there, she followed Mom and Dad to Germany after they retired. She's been involved in human rights and refugee causes in Munich for two years. Single, very attractive. I included some photos. And from what I can gather, lives a fairly liberated lifestyle."

"Meaning?"

"According to Facebook and Instagram she plays hard. And has a lot of interesting men passing through her life." He opened the file again, flipped through it and retrieved a photograph and tossed it on the table.

Harper picked up the photo. It looked more like a glamour shot than a simple Facebook profile image. Blonde and, yes, she was quite attractive with startlingly blue eyes, the high cheekbones of a cosmetics model. Her lips appeared to be enhanced.

"Any chance you came across a boyfriend who's Kurdish?"

"Again, this is the reason you pay me so well. A boyfriend with a Turkish passport. But he listed himself on a housing application as being Kurdish. The daughter listed him as a reference in an employment application with one of the NGOs working in the refugee camps in Iraq."

"Someone by the name of Murat?"

"Yeah, Murat something or other. Zorro. No. Zaro. I couldn't come up with much on him on any of the usual search sites. He's a ghost. Unemployed from what I can tell, but has a couple of credit cards with high limits. It seems he showed up in Berlin a year ago. Since then he stays under the radar, although I did come across an inquiry made by the German Federal Police. Which is probably not unusual for being a foreigner. It didn't seem to go anywhere. If you want, I can try to have a colleague in Germany find out more."

"Maybe later. Did you find out anything current on the situation in Kurdistan and northern Iraq?"

"There's a report in there I downloaded from State Department sites. Most of Iraqi Kurdistan should be safe. It may be a little iffy once you go into the other Iraqi provinces, but you already knew that. And you already know the closer you get to the Syrian border the worse it gets. I suspect the triangle area where the borders of Iraq, Turkey, Syria meet might be especially risky right now. Tell me, *chica*. You are not going there, are you?"

She gave a noncommittal shrug.

"You've watched the news. The Turks and Assad's forces are about to get into it. So far it's just been random shelling and skirmishes. But it won't be too long until the shit hits the proverbial fan. Regardless, around Mosul and along the border are the PMU, the Public Mobilization Units. A benign name for the Iraqi government sponsored Shia militias. Then you've got your regular Iraqi Army units, and the Kurdish Army, the Peshmerga. Throw in the anti-Assad Syrian Democratic Forces who are mostly Kurds that are retreating across the border into Iraq to get out of the way of both Assad and the Turks. And you can't forget the PKK, the Kurdish Workers' Party and their militias. They've been fighting Turkey for thirty-five years. Our government still lists them as a terrorist group. But again, you already know all that. A witch's brew, yes? But wait, there's more.

"There are apparently still some ISIS hiding in caves up in the mountains above Erbil. Sprinkle in Assad's Hezbollah militias that might wander across the border from Syria. And also you can bet there are some of our covert special ops types lurking around. Cross into Syria and you might even find some Spetsnaz, Russian Special Forces who are advising Assad's military. Are you still with me?"

"All right. Enough. You've warned me."

"I am just saying that there are many pissed off people wandering around with too many guns."

Harper snorted in amusement. "Jesus. That sounds just like the evening news."

"My invoice is on the first page. I've already scheduled another dental appointment. Oh, and I almost forgot. Ras al-Saumar. He's waiting to hear from you. He's in Mosul now. His email address is on the last page. And let me know if you want me to put you in contact with someone who can find out more. I have already left behind more tracks than I am comfortable with." Manny reached for his satchel and started to get up. "So, *Corazon.* You're not going back there, are you?"

"Not if I can help it. Thanks, Manny. I'll call you if I think of anything else."

Manny stood and came over and gave her a kiss on the cheek. "*Hasta la proxima vez,*" he said and turned and shuffled out,

She sat there a moment, digesting what she had learned. Knowing Manny, there was still a lot of material to go over. The only thing that stood out was that there seemed a lot more to Adele Marchand than met the eye. Like why she hadn't mentioned being on the embassy staff in Prague.

She would have to do some homework before deciding how deeply to get involved in all this. She sat there awhile longer, sipping her Americano and staring at nothing in particular, her mind slipping back to what had awakened her at dawn in the hotel room in Troy,

She picked up her laptop, turned it on, and started sorting through various files. It took a couple of minutes to find the one she was looking for. She scrolled down, hesitated and then clicked on a photo of Rodavan washing his car and giving Harper the thumbs up sign. In the background, Nadia and the children were playing on a swing set. She stared at the image for a long moment. She had never found out what happened to Nadia and the children. All of her efforts had come to naught. They had simply disappeared into the weft and warp of the war. Maybe a refugee center, or perhaps they had simply moved in with relatives. She stopped looking after a year.

Her finger hovered over another file. She hesitated for a couple of seconds before clicking it open. The photo had been taken by another journalist. It showed Harper and Luke sitting on a couple of camp stools outside the UN barracks in Sarajevo. She appeared exhausted, haggard, in spite of her beaming smile. Luke, as usual, posed with casual aplomb, his blue eyes sparkling in the bright fall sunlight. His closely cropped blonde hair framed a blocky, chiseled face. His wide mouth was formed into a toothy grin, almost a smirk that strangers found both disarming and discomforting. Giving into some wistful impulse, she stroked the image with her index finger for a moment before closing the laptop.

Her eyes fell on the thick binder Manny had left. All of her instincts, told her to toss it the nearest dumpster and walk away. Thanks to a decade of therapy, she was sufficiently self-aware to know she couldn't do that, wouldn't do that. Not until she finished reading Manny's report. Only then would she call Adele Marchand.

PART TWO

"No one leaves home unless home is in the mouth of a shark."
-Warsan Shire

7

DEIR EZ-ZOR, SYRIA
NOVEMBER 20TH

Maggie took one final drag off the cigarette, coughed, and tossed the butt into one of the muddy potholes that pockmarked the narrow rutted road. It had rained heavily earlier that afternoon, cleansing the air of the pungent, sulfurous smell of the nearby oil fields. The odor permeated everything; her clothes, her hair, their water, the food. Even the cigarettes reeked of oil. She knew she needed to quit, for the harsh Turkish tobacco triggered her asthma something fierce. When this pack is empty, she would stop, although she knew there was little chance of that happening.

The boredom and stress of moving to a different house every several days was beginning to wear on her. This last place was little more than a hut; one room with a curtained alcove where she and Murat slept. She was done with almost three weeks of Murat's excuses; done with Murat and his three companions. These are my cousins, Murat proclaimed the day they had all crossed the border together under the cover of darkness. Another so-called cousin hustled them off in the back of a sheep trailer. They were no more his cousins than the old woman and the two children sifting through the mud at the edge of the nearby ravine were gold miners.

She glanced self-consciously over her shoulder at her minder man perched on a rock on the other side of the rutted road. Murat wouldn't allow her to go anywhere without him. For your protection, he had said. This is dangerous country for a woman, especially a Westerner, he explained. The young man shadowing her every move seemed more a prison guard than a protector. Like a sheep dog, he steered her this way and that with a nod of his head. His name was Hassan, and ostensibly, Murat's first cousin. That fiction and the pretense of crossing into Syria to attend a family reunion had long since fallen by the wayside. Did Murat really believe she was that gullible?

Obviously he did, for she had naively bought into the whole fucking charade for far too long, she thought, muttering a curse. When they first arrived, Murat had assured her that it would merely be for a day or two before they would leave for the camps. That had been nearly a week ago. But there was always some excuse. The Syrian Army was nearby. Then it was the Turkish Army. The road to Kurdistan was probably mined. A safe house was no longer available.

Hadn't her mother warned her? And as usual, she had ignored what she thought was the same tired advice her mother had been offering since high school. Obviously, all of Adele's hectoring had been for naught. I should have a tattoo on my forehead that says 'bad choice in men', she thought bitterly. And for this boneheaded choice, she had only herself to blame.

She should've known something wasn't right when her iPad had suspiciously gone missing soon after they crossed the border into Syria. Murat admonished her for not concealing it better. Thieves are everywhere along the border, he told her. She accepted his explanation even though the iPad had been locked in a suitcase, Three days later, right after she had called her mother, her cell phone disappeared. She suspected Hassan, but without any proof, she foolishly let it go.

She found it all rather puzzling, if not disconcerting. The Murat she had known in Munich, the sweet, devil may care romantic who had wooed her had turned into a controlling, petty, tyrant. She had to admit it wasn't the first time she had been taken in by a manipulative suitor. Now every night she awoke at three AM and wondered whether she would end up in some Arabian cathouse. Did Murat really think she was sex trafficking material with her thick ankles, tiny breasts and too wide hips? Granted, she had a beautiful face. Ever since landing in Istanbul, her exotic blue eyes and alabaster complexion had drawn uncomfortable stares.

The abrupt change in Murat's personality only cemented her anxiety. They had last made love that first night after arriving in Istanbul, but ever since then any display of affection had dwindled by the day. And any attempt to ascertain the reason why had been met by at first denial, then diversion, and finally, a coldness bordering on contempt. There was no two ways about it. For whatever reason, she was now a captive.

She walked over to the muddy ravine to see what the old woman and the two young boys were doing. It took her a few moments to realize the three of them were making bricks. Using the end of a thick tree branch, one of the boys tamped bits of straw into the ravine's viscous mud bank, while the old woman scooped the mixture into a series of crude shoe-box sized molds that the other boy carefully overturned onto a tattered canvas tarp.

It had grown colder with the dwindling daylight, the low restless clouds threatened more rain. Instead of starting back, she turned and began to walk further down the road. Hassan hurried to catch her. As far as she could tell, he neither spoke nor understood even the most basic English. She even wondered about his Turkish. The few instances that she heard him and Murat speaking it sounded as if they were conversing in Arabic. She had picked up a smattering in both languages; at least enough to recognize which language was which. Enough to deem it unlikely they were cousins. And when she spoke to Hassan with the few words and phrases she knew in Kurdish it failed to elicit a response. Their spare communication was even more limited by his obviously dull intellect. A sheepdog displayed more savvy.

Hassan caught up and stepped in front of her. "*Yjb 'an taeud,*" he said, back peddling.

She offered him a smile. "Sorry, I don't understand your gibberish. Plus, you are a mental defective. Do you understand? You are an ignorant piece of shit," she said with unmitigated delight. He smiled and she shook her head and started to brush past him. He grabbed her by the wrist, spinning her around.

"Don't touch me!" she snarled, jerking away.

He raised his hands as if in apology, but stepped in front of her, blocking her way.

"Have it your way, you dick."

She spun on her heel and strode back in the direction of the house. She needed to finally have it out with Murat. This fairy tale about visiting the camps had gone on long enough. She found him in the rear of the house, shovel in hand. She couldn't tell if he was digging up something or burying it.

In spite of the cold, he had stripped to the waist, his doughy muscles visible beneath his boyish pudginess. He was handsome, she would give him that. Part of his appeal had always been the olive complexion, the dark, soulful eyes, the soft mouth of a cherub, and yes, his hands that caressed her as gently as if she were made of fine china.

He paused to take a drag from his cigarette before looking at her, and then resumed his digging.

"I want to go back to Istanbul. Now," she added when he offered no reaction.

"That is not possible. Tomorrow we leave for the camps."

"You told me that a week ago. Besides, I don't want to go to the camps anymore. I want to go back to Munich. I'm done with this. Done with you."

He didn't reply. Instead he continued to dig away at the muddy soil. She heard the shovel strike something that sounded metallic. He paused, leaned over the shallow hole and swiped at something.

"You should go in now," he said, looking up at her.

"I'm going home."

He stood and walked over to her. "You do as I say. Go in now."

"Why have you become such an asshole? I never would've..."

He struck her face with the back of his hand hard enough to almost make her lose her balance.

"You do not curse me. Do you understand?"

She touched her face and glared at him. "No, You understand. I'm not staying."

He started to raise his hand again but she raised her arm to block him. "Don't you dare! If you ever hit me again, you'll regret it," she said.

He smiled. "Ah, you Western women. It is what makes you so attractive." His smile disappeared. "Now go inside before I have Hassan drag you there."

She shook her head, partly in defiance, partly in confusion. "My god! Why, Murat? Why all this?"

"It is not for you to know. Now go and prepare us tea. One more thing. From now on you shall call me Emin."

She sneered and turned away. She needed to remember to spit in their tea.

The other two men were sprawled on a pair of cots, each perusing a magazine that appeared to be the Middle Eastern equivalent of Playboy. One of them, the slender, bookish one, turned his back to her. The other, the burly one with snide attitude, studied her over the top of the magazine as she walked over to the small cook stove. She tried to ignore him as she struggled to light the gas ring. Once the flame finally caught, she placed the tea kettle atop it, and peered out the window.

Murat was pulling what appeared to be a long metal footlocker from the hole he had dug. He brushed off the dirt and started to open it, but then looked up and saw her watching from the window. He looked at her a moment, and then with some effort, cradled the footlocker in his arms and disappeared around the corner of the house.

Enough of this, she decided. When they first arrived, she had paid close attention to the roads leading to the house. It was a habit ingrained in her by her father. You will never get lost if you know where you've been, Luke had always told her. Even though they had arrived in darkness, she took note of the roads leading to the oil fields. She had seen a sign for a road leading to a nearby Conoco refinery, its lights visible some distance from the house.

A plan began to form in her mind. Tonight, once they were all asleep, she would slip out and make her way to the refinery. The chances were that there would be someone there that might help her, a Western engineer maybe.

She went to the tiny anteroom she shared with Murat and began rummaging through her bag for her passport and credit cards. She rifled through all of her belongs, once, twice, and giving into panic, a third time. They were gone, just like her phone and iPad. There was no longer any sense confronting Murat. It only hardened her resolve to leave no matter what.

She sat there for a moment considering her options before picking up her cosmetics case. The bottle of Xanax was still there. She removed the five remaining tablets, slipped them into the pocket of her shirt, and went to make a pot of tea,

Murat stood at the sink, washing his hands. He barely glanced at her as she removed the pot of boiling water and poured it into the chipped ceramic tea kettle containing the loose tea leaves. For some reason, he stood there watching her every move. There would be no way she could dump the Xanax tablets into the kettle without him noticing.

"We're going to the camps tomorrow?" she asked with feigned cheerfulness. "You promise?"

He didn't reply at first. "Yes," he said finally. "We will cross the border into Iraq. There is a large camp. Bardarash. You will see what the camps are like."

"I want to stay there for a few days. At the camp. I promised the people in Munich I would observe and write a report."

Again, he merely looked at her but said nothing. After a moment, he turned and said something to the other two men who rather reluctantly rose and came to the table. Hassan was nowhere to be seen. She needed them all here to drink the tea. She started to fumble in her pocket for the tablets, but before she could retrieve them, Murat took the tea kettle and placed it on the table.

"Bring us our cups," he said harshly.

With her back turned to them, she removed the cups from the sink and made a show of drying them before taking the five tablets from her pocket. She had no other choice but to place a tablet in each of the cups as surreptitiously as possible and hope they didn't notice. She placed the cups on the table and quickly filled each of them.

Murat muttered a curse. "How many times must I tell you the tea needs to steep?"

"I'm sorry. I forgot," she said, handing Murat a cup. "If it is too strong you won't sleep. You said so yourself."

He glared at her, and then reached for the small bowl of sugar cubes. He dropped in three cubes and began to absently stir the tea. After a half-minute or so, he tossed the spoon on the table and raised the cup to his lips. He took a slip and then paused, lowered the cup an inch and peered into it. Taking up the spoon again, he wriggled it around in the cup, and then carefully removed it.

"What is this?" he asked, holding the spoon out to her.

The Xanax tab looked as if it hadn't dissolved even a little.

She looked at him but said nothing. He took the spoon and tilted it until the tablet dropped onto the table. He looked at her and smiled.

"I ask you again. What is this?"

"If you really want to know, it's rat poison."

He started to raise his hand as if to hit her and she pulled back. "Okay," she said. "It's Xanax. A sleeping pill."

He seemed to consider this a moment before delicately picking up the pill between his thumb and index finger. He studied it for a second or so and then smiled at her.

"Yes. You should sleep," he said, and then nodded and said something in Turkish to the burly one who had stood and was now leaning over the table to look at the tablet.

Before she could react, he lunged at her and encircled her in his arms. With one hand, he pulled her head back in a viselike grip. Murat leaned over her, and with his one hand, tried to force her jaws open. She tried to turn away, but couldn't. He forced her mouth open with his thumb and jammed the tablet into her mouth. She spit it back at him. He peeled the tablet off his shirt and again forced her mouth open. This time, he held her mouth closed after squeezing the tablet between her gritted teeth. With one hand over her nose, he held her until she had no choice but to swallow and gasp for air. He nodded at the other man to let her go as they both stepped back.

"Now you will sleep." He offered a smile. "I will tell you once more. My name is Emin. You will no longer call me Murat. Now, you will go to bed or I will have my friends take you there. You understand?"

She swiped the blood from her lips and stood up. Without looking at either of them, she walked into the small bedroom and dropped onto the bed. The next morning she couldn't remember ever falling asleep.

Emin needed to calm himself. He walked outside and lit one of the special Turkish cigarettes he carefully hoarded, the ones laced with hashish. He took a long drag of the pungent smoke and stared up at the sky. In the distance, he could see the flares of the gas wells and the lights of the nearby refinery. There was still talk in the tea houses and war rooms of Istanbul that Turkey should take advantage of the Syrian civil war and annex these oil fields, the prevailing argument being who would stop them; not Iraq, not Assad, not the West. It was simply a matter of patience, the autocrats said. Patience and the further disintegration of Damascus's control of the north. And to that end, he had been given his role. If he was successful, he

62

would parlay his achievement with another plum assignment in the West. He relished the more liberated and freer atmosphere of places like Munich or Paris. Perhaps he might even be sent to London.. He found Western women were high-spirited, the lifestyle more suitable to his tastes.

But the plan seemed to be going to shit, he thought, taking one more drag before extinguishing the joint with his fingers. He had been told initially that his contact would meet up with him in a village just outside of Al Qāmishli. Then the meeting had been abruptly changed to a hostel just outside of the nearby oil refinery. And then last night came a new communication ordering him to meet up with the contact in the south instead, in a small village near a town called Abū Kamāl. The original plan called for completing the exchange and then slipping across the border through the oil fields and into Iraq. Now it meant traveling a far greater distance to the south, all the while risking encounters with Assad's allies, the Hezbollah militias. Then, once in Iraq, they would have to dodge the Shia militias and the Iraqi Army. The risk to success ratio had suddenly changed dramatically.

And now there was the woman to enter into the equation. Beforehand, his efforts to deceive her had proved simple. But the constant changing of safe houses, the lame excuses he had been forced to make, only served to raise both her suspicions and her ire. Now, much to his dismay, she had become an unwilling, distrustful captive. It would no longer be a simple matter of using her to gain entrance to the camp under the false pretense of inspecting the camp. Now, she had suddenly become a liability. Yet she still might have some use, so he was reluctant to discard her quite yet. It just meant concealing her from prying eyes.

He walked over to the truck and raised the lid of the footlocker. At first, he had been reluctant to attempt crossing into Iraq with a stash of weapons. Now he realized he might very well need them. In the morning, he would brief the men as to the revised mission plan. He knew there was no point in downplaying the risks. Of course, none of them knew the exact nature of the mission, only that they had been tasked to escort him into

Iraq, and later back across the Turkish frontier. At some point, they would all be expendable, especially the driver Jamal. From the onset, Emin had questioned why he had been saddled with someone like Jamal who seemed more a errand boy than a covert operative. He felt much the same about the inept, thick-headed Hassan. Only after a full briefing had it become clear why Hassan had been chosen, for he was the only one with a Syrian passport.

As always, the hashish made him languid and reflective. His thoughts turned back to Maggie. It was rather unfortunate that it had come to this, for he had unwillingly allowed himself to grow fond of her. She had proven to be an exciting companion, passionate, though naive, but also unlike many Western women, curious and accepting of his culture. He had initially targeted her for no other reason than her affiliation with refugee relief organizations. However, when his current assignment had been revealed, he initially balked, partially because of his affinity for her, no matter how superficial, but also because of Maggie's mother. He knew of her background. That coupled with her strenuous objections to their traveling to Kurdistan would undoubtedly raise her suspicions.

He felt a stab of remorse at what he had just done to Maggie, as well as for the earlier episode when he had slapped her. At the time, he had felt he had no choice for he saw Hassan watching them, and had no doubt Hassan would make mention to the others if Emin had been seen allowing a Western woman to berate him. He reminded himself that he had committed greater transgressions against women when necessary, not that it gave him any comfort. He tried to convince himself there still might be a way out for her, all the while realizing his task required that no one be left behind to bear witness. With this heavy on his mind, he went back inside.

8

MOSUL, IRAQ
NOVEMBER 21ST

Luke pulled to a stop fifty yards or so before the gate and allowed himself to take in the layout. He had been on high alert ever since entering Mosul, his vigilance a deeply ingrained habit. As he drove through the debris-cluttered streets, he scrutinized his surroundings for every possible hazard, profiling every suspicious loiterer, checking out the gaping windows in the few houses still standing, every derelict vehicle a potential ambush. At one time, these precautions might have meant the difference between life and death. But he had left that life over a decade ago, and now such safeguards seemed nothing more than a vestigial paranoia that had long since outlived its wartime utility.

Most, if not all, of the buildings in the city had sustained major damage, and many of the streets were still clogged with rubble. Crude fences of corrugated tin and barbed wire encircled many of the ruins. Here and there still sat burned out vehicles, many sporting growths of weeds from their windows, the weeds the only obvious greenery. Even the Tigris appeared muddy and derelict. He had stopped at one point to survey what remained of the Great Mosque of al-Nuri. A mountain of broken stone marked where the al-Hadba', the famous leaning minaret, had once stood. A fragment of its latticed base was the only feature still recognizable.

Pre-war accounts portrayed Mosul as a bustling, picturesque city on the Tigris with a population of just under two million. It had been an important military center under Saddam Hussein. The city had also been home to libraries and a university. The banks of the emerald green Tigris had been lined with coffee houses. Now sixteen years of war had left it a decrepit shadow of its previous self. The recent ISIS occupation and the subsequent year-long campaign to liberate the city by the Iraqi and Peshmerga armies had been the final blow. What was the adage from the Vietnam War? "We had to destroy the city in order to save it." So it now stood as just another war ravaged collection of bombed out buildings amid piles of rubble.

Yasin had assured him GPS would be of little use in finding the site of his warehouse and office. Instead, he provided Luke with detailed directions that still proved useless due to the lack of landmarks or street signs. Consequently, it had taken over an hour of meandering through the maze of naked streets asking the occasional clueless passersby before he finally located Yasin's warehouse.

Yasin Rahal had once been a colonel in Saddam Hussein's Army. After the American liberation, he had deftly switched allegiance with almost maniac alacrity, maintaining his rank in the new Iraqi Army. He and Luke had worked hand in hand on various joint operations, forming a friendship based on mutual respect and trust; a trust that had become strained if not broken after the incident that ended Luke's military career. However, when the time came to seek assistance in finding local support in his search for Maggie, Luke had little choice but to put aside his reservations and residual rancor and reach out to Yasin.

He slipped the Land Cruiser into gear and drove toward a couple of large Quonset style warehouses surrounded by several acres of pallets of lumber and steel panels. The guard at the entrance waved him down and casually approached Luke's window. He wore rumpled, mismatched combat fatigues and a New York Yankees baseball cap. A sawed-off Remington shotgun hung from his shoulder. Luke handed him his passport and removed his sunglasses.

"I'm Luke Marchand. I'm here to see Yasin Rahal." He repeated his own name twice to make sure the guard had heard it correctly. He regretted not keeping up his limited Arabic.

The guard kept shifting his eyes from the passport photo to Luke's face in an attempt to reconcile the difference in the two images. Luke could excuse the guard's puzzlement, for the passport photo was eight years old. At the time, Luke still wore his hair in a military buzz cut and was clean shaven. The man the guard scrutinized in the Land Cruiser was noticeably older with a four day-old growth of beard and dirty blonde hair worn stylishly long over his ears and the collar of his windbreaker.

The guard eventually handed him back his passport and pointed to a double-wide trailer parked just inside the gate. A silver 5 Series BMW sedan sat parked in front. Along beside it were parked two olive drab Humvees. Luke parked behind the BMW and then sat for a moment to collect his thoughts. He hadn't seen or spoken to Yasin since the day he had been abruptly recalled back to Fort Benning to face the inquiry. Their parting had been uncomfortable to say the least. Luke wondered how and if the incident that had broken their bond would be broached. In the end, he decided to leave the ball in Yasin's court.

Another guard waited at the top of the wooden stairway. He had obviously been alerted to Luke's arrival as he greeted Luke with a crisp salute before ushering him inside. The office's interior was tricked out in plush white shag carpet and expensive looking but somewhat gauche flocked red wall paper. A large and ornately-framed velvet image of the Great Mosque hung on a wall above a ten foot long leather sofa. Two window-mounted air conditioning units rattled and hummed loudly on either side of the sofa. Yasin sat talking on the phone behind a mahogany desk the size of a large dining room table. He gestured for Luke to sit as he barked what sounded like orders to someone on the other end. After a minute, he abruptly hung up and rose from behind the desk to greet Luke.

"Lucas. My friend," he shouted. "At last."

The two of them embraced each other with the usual backslapping and faux kisses on each cheek. Luke studied his old comrade at arm's length. Yasin had grown older and fatter, his jowls hanging loosely over the collar of his shirt. His eyes had the glassy, blood shot look of someone who couldn't wait until the end of the day for their first drink. When Luke had known him before, Yasin was a stalwart Muslim and a teetotaler, at least so in public.

"Come, sit. We will drink some arak and catch up."

He produced a large bottle of the anise flavored liquor along with a bowl of olives from a small refrigerator behind his desk. With an exaggerated flourish, he poured them each a glass of arak and leaned back in his chair.

"*Fe sahatek,*" Yasin said raising his glass in a toast before quickly downing it in one swallow. "What do you think?" he asked, spreading his arms effusively. "Did you ever think I would be… how do you call it? A captain of industry?"

"It looks like you're doing well for yourself. It doesn't surprise me."

A long moment of uncomfortable silence followed. Yasin poured himself another drink and pushed the plate of olives across the desk. Yasin downed the glass of arak and held out the bottle to Luke.

"No thanks," Luke said, hoisting his glass and taking a sip of the warm, sweetish liquor. "I won't take up too much of your time. I need a driver who speaks English, preferably someone who can handle difficult situations."

"You mean someone who can get you past roadblocks without being harassed or shot? Is that what you require?"

"Maybe more than that."

"May I ask why you need someone with such talents?"

Luke took another sip of the arak. "My daughter is missing. She could be here in northern Iraq. Possibly even in Syria."

Yasin shook his head. "Missing you say? But you don't know exactly where? This does sound difficult."

"I want to go to the refugee camps first. She was planning on inspecting them."

"There are many such camps."

"I realize that. I would like someone who speaks Arabic and Kurdish."

Yasin thought for a moment and then nodded. "I believe I know of such a man. I used him to settle a labor dispute I had with some Kurdish workers. A former soldier. Perhaps he is the sort of man you seek." He reached for a notebook, opened it, and after a minute paging through it, took a piece of paper and wrote something down. "He calls himself Masoud. A rough sort of fellow but reliable I believe." He handed Luke the slip of paper. "I did not expect to see you again," he said, pushing his chair back.

Luke finished the arak and carefully set it on the desk. "Tell me something. The house my men raided. Did you know there would be women and children there?"

Yasin looked at him for a moment before replying. "I told you. It was the home of a Ba'athist pig who was responsible for killing Americans. Your men. He was a general in Saddam's Army, and then an insurrectionist. You knew that."

"And you were a colonel in Saddam's Army."

"Yes, and I wasn't killing your men."

"You didn't answer my question, Yasin."

"It was war. Innocents are sometimes killed."

"Innocents? And he was never there."

"You know yourself that you often receive bad intelligence."

"I heard later that this so called Ba'athist pig owned a factory. A factory you were trying to seize."

"You should not believe everything you are told. What does your President call such things? Fake news?"

Luke knew he would never get to the truth, not that it made any difference. It was the way of the world, especially in a place like Iraq. Besides, that life was behind him. Now he had to focus on Maggie, He picked up the paper and looked at it.

"Thanks for this. And the drink." He rose to his feet. "Tell me one thing. Whatever happened to this Ba'athist?"

Yasin shrugged. "He was killed in a car bomb along with his wife, unfortunately." He started to say something and then started over. "I am sorry for what happened." He stood and extended his hand.

Luke hesitated a moment before taking Yasin's hand. "You won't see me again," he said and walked out.

9

BARDARASH REFUGEE CAMP
NORTHERN IRAQ

Luke leaned forward from his slumping position in the front seat of the
Land Cruiser and slipped his glasses down from his forehead to better see
the sudden mass of people flooding through the nearby line of tents. Their
apparent destination seemed to be a trio of tractor trailers parked in a row
along the fence. They appeared to be mostly women, all of them either carrying pails or clutching cardboard boxes. The ration line, he assumed. He
studied them for a moment before turning his gaze back to Masoud who
appeared to be in deep in conversation with the two soldiers manning the
gate. The soldiers wore well-tailored, bluish and black camouflage fatigues
accessorized with the requisite web gear and lethal weaponry. They looked
like the Peshmerga troops he had seen in Erbil, but the camp was, theoret-
ically at least, outside of Kurdish jurisdiction.

They looked much different than the poorly dressed guards he had
encountered at one of the camps he had visited the previous day. That particular camp seemed more of a temporary harbor, the tents makeshift and
less uniform. The two gate sentries were both somewhat elderly and obviously civilians pressed into guard duty. One clutched what appeared to be
a World War II vintage rifle of some sort, the other one armed only with
what appeared to be a policeman's night stick.

It called to mind several Western movies Luke had seen as a child. The ones where all the peace-loving mercantile types and townspeople arm themselves with whatever they can find in order to back up the solitary, granite-jawed sheriff who was usually played by someone like Gary Cooper or maybe Rory Calhoun. Except Luke never saw anyone in the camp that resembled a sheriff, only a bunch of desperate, ill-clothed old men cradling mismatched weapons.

Bardarash was the fourth and the largest camp he had visited in as many days. It had been much the same at each one of them. An overwhelmed and irritable administrator for some NGO Luke had never heard of who was adamant, even defensive, that no one matching Maggie's description had been at their camp. And Luke had just as adamantly demanded to walk through the camp to see for himself.

Nothing of what he saw shocked him. He had experienced firsthand these sorts of places in Bosnia, then later in Iraq. He had always bore stoic witness to the squalor and despair, but always managed at day's end to shed the desolation like a dirty shirt. Or so he liked to think. It was always later, when he lay in his cot or sat slumped in some sandbagged hooch, that he had time to reflect on the sorry state of mankind. This often called to mind something his father, a professor of philosophy, liked to spout while perusing his morning newspaper. "Man is a wolf to man. The Roman playwright Plautus," he would add while giving Luke a querying glance, testing him as it were. Luke's reply was invariably glib, something to the effect of 'Yeah, Dad. I saw the movie'. Luke turned his glance back to the flood of people grouped around the trucks.

"Man is a wolf to man. No shit," he murmured, and allowed himself a smile at the memory of his father and his tired platitudes. The old man had been sorely disappointed that Luke had rejected a life of academia to become a soldier. In fact, his bitterness regarding Luke's career choice followed his father to the grave. Masoud interrupted his thoughts as he flung open the door and hurled himself behind the steering wheel.

"They say they have not seen the woman you describe. They say you should ask the UN person," he said, nodding at a double-wide trailer parked just beyond the first line of tents.

Masoud had showed up at Luke's hotel the day after his meeting with Yasin. The Kurd claimed to be forty but looked at least two decades older. He had a shock of shoulder length gray hair although his bushy eyebrows and beard were coal black. Luke knew from experience that dyeing one's beard and eyebrows black was a common practice in this part of the world.

Masoud was a Syrian Kurd and a veteran of years of soldiering, first with the PKK in their guerilla war with Turkey, and later in the war to liberate Kurdistan from Saddam Hussein, he was terse and sober, attributes Luke found to be common amongst combat veterans. The Kurd eschewed any kind of military garb, dressing instead in baggy trousers and the same emerald green Notre Dame sweatshirt topped off with a frayed, navy blue pea coat. Any reservations Luke might have harbored dissipated their first day on the road when they encountered a Shia militia roadblock just outside of Mosul.

The Shia militiamen wore an assortment of cast-off uniforms, their only nod to conformity their head bands proclaiming their allegiance to the prophet Ali ibn Abi Talib, something that Masoud remarked on with barely concealed scorn before dismounting from the Land Rover. The militiamen's initial bluster in attempting to discern why he and Luke deigned to pass through their roadblock was met with equal bluster on the Kurd's part. A war of words and attempts at intimidation followed as a trio of militiamen surrounded Masoud while another manhandled Luke from the SUV. The conflict only escalated when Luke was forced to show his US passport. A tense five minute standoff ensued while Masoud gesticulated and derided their antagonists. The situation was defused only by the appearance of their likely superior who after taking a quick glance at Luke's passport, motioned for them to be on their way,

As they drove off, Masoud seemed to shrug off the whole episode as he launched into a dispassionate monologue detailing what he thought needed to be done in regards to these militias soiling Kurdistan's lands. Luke realized then that the unflappable Masoud was the right man for the job.

Masoud pulled the SUV off to the side and they both got out and began walking past the refugees lined in front of the supply trucks. On closer inspection, Luke saw that most of the refugees were indeed women, and older women at that. A few were quite young, several of them obviously pregnant. None of them seemed to pay Luke and Masoud any mind, their faces reflecting a weary stoicism. It had grown colder overnight, the sky a fish gray canvas of ragged clouds. The clerk at the hotel in Erbil said there would be snow tonight in the mountains to the north. Few of the refugees appeared dressed for the weather. Some wore only house slippers and threadbare shawls.

The double-wide trailer displayed an official looking metal sign that simply stated United Nations High Commissioner for Refugees ADMIN. Below that was printed something in Arabic and some other language, Kurdish he assumed. A bearded young man with dark, shoulder length hair sat on a stool at the entrance, his attention focused on a clipboard that he flipped through with only cursory attention. He looked up at them and stopped them with an open hand.

"Yes? What is it you need?" he asked in a heavy Germanic accent.

"*Ich würde gern den Administrator sehen,*" Luke replied in halting German, hoping to score points.

The man studied Luke for a moment. "*Dein Geschäft?*"

"*Ich suche jemanden.* I'm looking for someone," he repeated in English, figuring he had exhausted his German fluency.

"A refugee? Or a worker?" The man already appeared bored, his attention focused back on the clipboard. He wore a greasy looking military fatigue jacket. One could see the darker areas where the insignias had been removed from the sleeves and above the pockets.

"Neither really. A visitor. Someone who might have passed through on an inspection tour, perhaps," he said, hoping to lend the weight of officialdom.

The man didn't reply at first, all the while consulting his clipboard. After a moment, he looked up and gestured with his head for them to go inside.

"I wait," Masoud said, stepping away and lighting a cigarette.

The trailer's interior smelled of disinfectant and cigarette smoke, and felt even colder than outside. The young woman sitting at a desk next to the doorway was shouting in what sounded like Arabic at someone over the phone. She wore a heavy sweater and gloves, the kind with the fingertips exposed. She paid Luke only the slightest attention as he stood there looking around for someone who might be in charge. In the rear of the trailer were three desks, one much larger than the other two, all of them occupied by women. Going by the size of the desk and a hunch, Luke assumed its tenant was the person he was looking for.

As he approached the desk, the woman looked up, gave him a dismissive glance, and turned her attention back to the papers scattered across the desk top.

Luke cleared his throat. "Excuse me."

She flicked down her heavy, black-rimmed glasses and looked at him. She had a long, horsey face topped with an unflattering, closely cropped platinum hairstyle that revealed gray roots. He guessed her to be somewhere in her fifties, her fair complexion sun worn and creased. She studied him for a moment before reaching for the half-smoked cigarette at her elbow.

"Yes. What can I do for you?" she asked, the 'you' shortened to a 'ya'. She sounded like she might be Australian. She spoke with her mouth closed, her thin knife-like lips quickly parting to accept her cigarette. She took a long drag, tilting her head and closing one eye. Her eyes were a washed out, watery blue, the lids puffy.

"Are you the person in charge, Miss...?" he asked scanning the desk and the wall behind her for anything that might reveal her name.

She stared at him, ignoring his question.

"I'm looking for someone who might've visited your camp. Her name's Maggie… Magdalena Marchand."

"Visited? Might I ask in what capacity?"

"She works with a refugee relief organization in Munich. She would've come through here sometime in the past several weeks. She wanted to see the conditions for herself."

The woman studied Luke for a moment before replying. "I don't think so. At least I would know about it if she had. You've checked the other camps?"

Luke nodded. "Is it possible she's here amongst the refugees?"

"And tell me why in bloody hell would she do that? I would think she would've spoken with us, don't you see? That is unless she truly wanted to know firsthand how the other half lives without benefit of my hospitality." A hint of a smile creased her thin lips.

Luke cast his glance around the room at the two young women huddled over their desks on either side. They both had the uneasy look of idealistic millennials who had by now come to the realization they would rather be back partying on campus.

"She's twenty-seven. Blonde. Five six, Maggie's her name," he said loud enough to get the young women's attention.

One of them looked up at him before shifting her gaze to the woman behind the desk.

"And why is it that you are looking for this young woman?"

"I'm her father. She hasn't called in two, almost three weeks."

The woman took another drag of her cigarette before grinding it out in a grimy ashtray that appeared not to have been emptied in quite some time. "No word in almost three weeks, you say?" She looked down at her desk as if searching for something she had misplaced. She looked to the side as if measuring her thoughts.

"Her father," she said dully and reached for another cigarette from the pack at her elbow. She shook one out, and rolled it between her fingers as if she were reconsidering lighting it.

"Yesterday, a group of refugees brought with them the body of a young woman they found beside the roadway not far from here. She's Caucasian. At least the best we can tell. No ID. I'm not saying…" She glanced down at her desk before looking back up.

Luke exhaled as if someone had punched him in the gut. He studied the various charts on the wall behind the woman's desk for a long moment before lowering his eyes.

"She had a tattoo. A crescent moon and some stars just inside her thigh. Her right thigh," Luke added, struggling to maintain his composure.

"Mr. Marchand, was it? You must realize…" She paused, tossing the unlit cigarette on the desk "Our doctor believes she has been dead for a couple of days at least. There's some decomposition. And there were injuries. We have obtained a fingerprint and a tissue sample while awaiting any inquiries. We had planned on dealing with her remains later today."

"I want to see her."

The woman started to reply and then hesitated. "Very well." She rose to her feet and for the first time Luke was able to appreciate her fully. She was long limbed and quite thin. As she stepped around the desk, he noticed her limp. She pulled a blue down jacket bearing the UNHCR logo from a hook on the wall and turned to the door without bothering to see if Luke followed. She paused on the stoop outside the trailer to slip on the jacket. It had grown colder and the low hanging clouds had begun to spit sleet that rattled the side of the trailer.

"It's this way," she said and started off down the line of tents without bothering to wait.

There was something about the way she walked that tugged at Luke's memory. It came to him as the woman stepped stiffly over some tent lines.

She has an artificial leg, he realized. She turned to wait for him, and most likely due to practiced intuition, sensed him studying her right leg.

She propped her right foot on top of a tent peg and lifted her pants leg to reveal the chrome metal device where her foot and ankle should have been. "I was a pilot. Royal Aussie Air Force. A rocket got us flying cargo into Khandahar. I was lucky. Just my lower leg. I recognized your look. Don't feel bad. I'm used to it. Where did you serve?"

"82nd Airborne. I remember Khandahar."

She nodded. "I'm Lizzie McDermott." She flicked her eyes away for a second before fixing them back on Luke. There was something in her gaze, a melancholia that Luke also recognized all too well. "Are you ready?" she asked.

Luke nodded and followed her as she shuffled her way deeper into the canvas-cloaked maze of tents.

10

They walked along in silence down a muddy track lined with what seemed endless but orderly rows of dingy white tents. Here and there were small clots of men sitting in front of the blazing 55 gallon drums that served as camp fires, smoking their cigarettes and engaging in muted conversation. They all appeared older for the most part, their faces reflecting the contentment of men allowed to idle the afternoon away as the women shopped for groceries. More than a few had cell phones pressed to their ear.

"Last count we had over sixteen thousand souls here, and more every bloody day. You're lucky the wind is blowing from the north. The dunnies. The latrines," she explained, nodding over her shoulder.

After a minute or so, she cut between some tents and led Luke to an enclosure at the bottom of a slope that rose up to the camp's edge. Razor wire had been strung haphazardly along the top of the cyclone fence that encircles the enclosure. It contained a lone Quonset hut and a couple of small sheds. A slender young man wearing civilian clothes sat at the gate, a rifle cradled in his arms. McDermott nodded to him as she approached, and he arose to unfasten the locked gate. She led Luke around the back of the Quonset hut to a small attached shed, its walls consisting of rusted corrugated steel panels. A sheet of plywood covered with a blue UN tarp served as its roof. The doorway was nothing more than a cyclone wire gate hung haphazardly on its hinges. She reached into her shirt and pulled out a thin cable necklace that held a handful of keys, leaned into the lock and unfastened the chain securing the gate.

"Here," she said, handing him a surgical mask from a box on a shelf just inside the entrance. "You'll want some of this on your mask." She held up a small bottle of some kind of viscous liquid. "Oil of wintergreen." She sprinkled a few drops onto her mask before tucking the mask's straps behind her ears and ducking inside. Luke did the same and followed her into the dim interior.

The wintergreen did little to conceal the pungently sebaceous smell of rot. McDermott pushed a sheet of plywood to the side to allow the gray afternoon light to expose the cramped interior. One wall held stacked crates labeled electrolyte solution. Folds of tattered and soiled canvas covered whatever else the shed held including what lay on a low wooden table in the shed's center. McDermott leaned over the crude table and unceremoniously yanked back the canvas sheet exposing an olive drab blanket. Luke saw no need to guess as to the nature of the shapeless form beneath it.

This time, McDermott peeled back the blanket with the delicacy a mother might use when uncovering her child. The plastic opaqueness of the flimsy body bag left little to the imagination as to its contents. McDermott looked at him as if awaiting his permission and then unzipped the top of the bag.

The smell overpowered him. It wasn't a smell foreign to him. But one he had never grown accustomed to either. He allowed himself a sharp intake of breath as he studied the bloated, misshapen face. Someone had made an effort to clean as much blood as possible from her facial wounds, but even then the corpse's features appeared battered beyond recognition. Her dirty blonde hair was matted with blood and bits of grass and twigs.

McDermott hesitated a moment before zipping the bag open further, exposing the woman's breasts and chest. Luke lowered his gaze, clutching at his dispassion as he studied the body. There were several raw looking wounds above her left breast that might have been knife wounds. Maggie's breasts were smaller he thought with mild discomfort. But then again, the corpse appeared so bloated that he couldn't be sure.

McDermott zipped the bag down to the dead woman's thighs before picking up a pair of latex gloves from a pile at the head of the table. She slipped them on, snapping them in place, and then held her hands up in front of her much like a surgeon about to enter the OR.

"Inside right upper thigh, you said?" she muttered through her mask.

Luke nodded and looked away. He could hear a sucking sound as McDermott pried the woman's legs apart. He allowed his eyes to drift down just long enough to see the mottled gray thighs were smeared with mud and dried blood. He pressed the mask to his nose and looked away.

"I don't see any tattoos," McDermott said. "See for yourself."

He shook his head, awash with a mixture of relief and revulsion. As he turned to leave, he heard McDermott zip the bag back up before stripping off her gloves. Outside, the sunlight, no less fierce for its lateness, momentarily blinded him. He blinked at the low hills in the distance, their summits shrouded by slanting gray clouds. McDermott joined him a moment later.

"Smoke?" she asked offering him a pack of Dunhills.

"No thanks. I…" A memory of Maggie strapped in a car seat flickered in his mind. "I gave it up. When we adopted Maggie," he felt compelled to add.

She nodded in some sort of understanding.

"I must apologize for her appearance. The girls and I were planning on cleaning her up, then wrap her in something decent and bury her later today. It doesn't sound right to say it was good timing on your part. I mean, to make sure it wasn't her. Your daughter."

"Who do you suppose she is?"

"We're not aware of any missing aid workers. I guess we'll wait and see if someone like you comes again to inquire. If not…" McDermott shrugged. "Either way, we'll give her a decent burial this afternoon if the weather holds. Come with me," she said, turning to walk up the slope. "I want to show you something."

Luke followed her up the sloping hillside towards a crude observation tower that overlooked the camp's fenced border. The weathered wooden ladder looked as if it hadn't been used in a while, but they nevertheless made it to the top without incident. From here, one could see the entirety of the camps and the low hills beyond. Even with the wind, a pall of smoke clung to the camp. Oddly enough, the smoke seemed the only sign of human activity.

"How many did you say? Sixteen thousand?"

McDermott leaned away from the wind to light her cigarette, took a long drag, and shook her head. "We're never really sure. I'd guess it's more like twenty by now. Taking a census isn't easy. They're Syrians, mostly. The UN estimates there are 245,000 refugees in Iraq alone."

Luke shook his head in amazement. "And this place is as big as a small city."

"It's like one of those frontier boom towns. It wasn't even here a year ago. Yeah, it is a city, and in a lot of ways life goes on here just like in any other city. Births, weddings, deaths, the day to day business of living. Meals get made. Babies fed. There're the usual arguments and reconciliations. People fall in love. Out of love." She took a puff of her cigarette. "One besotted night, I had a mind to make a sign to hang at the gate. The City of Refuge," she said with a grand dramatic swipe of her hand before going on. "I doubt either of us can quite imagine what kind of shit happens to make you give up on your home. Makes you strap your sprogs onto your back, bundle up the heirlooms, and walk days on miserable end to settle here."

Luke nodded. "I guess it's the price they pay for not having to worry about an artillery round coming through your roof."

It suddenly brought to mind a photograph that Harper Harris had presented him with. It depicted a woman and two small children squatting in the rubble of a bombed out house. He kept the photo in his desk drawer, occasionally taking it out and studying it in a fit of misplaced nostalgia,

"Not too long after I came here, I realized that we're all refugees. All of us in some state of exile."

"How do you figure?"

She took a pull from her cigarette. "Everyone in this godforsaken place... the aid workers, those girls back in my office. All of them seem to have left something behind. Everyone running from something, or to something. Take me for instance. I came here to get away from a failed marriage and my opioid addiction. Maybe that seems quite trivial compared to what these people are running from. We all come to a place like this, a place where we don't belong, a place where we don't want to be. But we don't have a choice but to become exiles," she said, glancing at him as if seeking affirmation.

"You won't get an argument there," he said.

"So what will you do?" she asked after a moment had passed.

"Keep looking. There's at least one more camp I haven't been to. I hear there're still some camps in Syria."

McDermott arched her eyebrows, but didn't comment.

"My driver suggested we go to Duhok. He says a lot of NGO types from the nearby camps go there for R & R. Maybe someone there has seen her. If not, I'll just scope out the countryside."

"I'm sure there's no point in telling you it's pretty daft out in the bush."

He nodded and then offered her his hand. She stabbed the cigarette between her lips and took his hand in both of hers.

"I'm glad it wasn't her," she said. "But... Do you have a cell number? In case... You know, if I hear of her."

"Of course." He tore a slip of paper from the small pad he kept in his pocket, jotted the number and handed it to her. "I should go."

"Be safe, Mr. Marchand."

He glanced once more at the camp, and then turned and made his way down the ladder, leaving Liz McDermott alone to survey her domain.

11

DUHOK, NORTHERN IRAQ

By the time they reached the outskirts of Duhok it was near dusk. The wind had picked up, kicking up swirls of dust that further obscured the hills surrounding the city. An occasional brief spit of sleet promised a further deterioration in the weather. The streets appeared crowded with cars, buses, every type of truck, and despite the weather, cyclists, many of which lumbered along with a passenger or two in tow. Rush hour, Luke thought as he tried to gain a sense of the city. He thought of the destruction he had seen in Mosul. In contrast, Duhok, a city only a little over an hour's drive to the north, appeared to have escaped the brunt of the war relatively unscathed.

Even though Masoud had chosen a less busy secondary road, they still encountered two additional check points at the border crossing into Dukok Province. The exit point was manned by Iraqi Army regulars who paid only cursory attention to their papers and quickly waved them through. At the entry checkpoint just outside of the city, Masoud knew one of the Peshmerga soldiers, having fought alongside him with the PKK back in the day. From what Luke could tell they exchanged the usual 'How are you? What are you doing with yourself?' type pleasantries before Luke sensed their conversation grew somber. As they drove off, Luke asked Masoud about their conversation. Masoud was silent for a moment before revealing that the soldier's two brothers had been killed in the fighting in Syria.

"Did you know them?"

"Yes. One of them, the younger. You have been a soldier?" He asked Luke after a moment of silence had passed.

"Yeah. Almost thirty years in the infantry. You know infantry?"

Masoud nodded,

Luke proceeded to provide a brief narrative of his years in the military. He could tell that what followed was an immediate reappraisal of him in the way Masoud glanced at him, as if there was suddenly a shared bond, an unspoken intimacy common to veterans of combat.

Once they arrived in the city, Masoud dropped Luke at a hostel, informing him that he would meet him for breakfast the next morning at a nearby eatery. Luke didn't ask where he was going and Masoud didn't volunteer. As he arranged for his room, a pair of Germans, a young man and a woman, both carrying large backpacks, entered the small foyer. Knowing Germans, it didn't surprise him when he overheard them tell the clerk they had been trekking in the mountains along the Iranian and Turkish border. With nothing to lose, he asked them whether by any chance they had encountered a woman matching Maggie's description but drew a blank.

He took a lukewarm shower in the phone booth-sized bathroom, changed into clean jeans and a sweater, and then settled atop the flimsy mattress to check his iPhone. There was another message from Adele imploring him to call.

Part of his reticence in calling her was due to the simple fact that he had nothing to report. But there was also a part of him that resisted calling her out of a passive-aggressive retribution stemming from his anger over her failing to notify him of Maggie's plans. In addition, he suspected she was being less than candid about what she really knew, for her evasiveness often seemed her second nature. For many years, he had accepted this attribute as a result of the nature of her job. But with time, it seemed to become more and more her modus operandi. The sad fact was they were both guilty of evasion, and in the end it had eroded the last vestige of their affection for each other. Still, like many failed marriages, there always remained a shred of that warm sense of what once was.

One night while on a motorcycle trip through Spain, he shared a drink at a bar with a man a decade or so older who had recently left a long marriage. The man, a frank talking Scotsman, had cynically compared a fading marriage to a favorite coat you hang onto even after realizing it no longer fits your girth or your needs. The more Luke thought about it the less cynical the Scotsman's take had sounded.

Adele had once told him he was a good man, a passable father, and a terrible husband. He retorted by admitting simply that she had been a good mother. And upon that evidence they went to trial, so to speak, the verdict of divorce a foregone and unanimous conclusion.

Back at Bardarash, when faced with the possibility of the ultimate tragedy, he had cringed at the prospect of having to inform Adele. Maggie had been their demilitarized zone, their only link to what had once been. Adele loved Maggie. For all her faults, she had always been a good mother. That bond seemed the only honest thing in their family's dysfunctional triad. Losing Maggie would devastate her. To his surprise, he suddenly felt an overwhelming empathy for Adele. Yet, the distance between them never felt greater.

For some reason, he thought of Liz McDermott's observation that everyone seemed to be fleeing something, exiles from something other than just one's homeland. The abrupt truth of her sentiment stung him, in spite of the fact he had fought that realization to a draw on more than one occasion. The therapist he and Adele had once consulted had suggested as much, outright asserting that Luke's melancholia stemmed from the fact he was anchorless; exiled from his lifetime career, exiled from a marriage that was floundering. Even his relationship with Maggie felt stagnant. All too often their time spent together seemed an afterthought. No matter where he turned, he seemed to be in some state of exile.

He put this thought aside as he deleted Adele's message, but then out of some unconscious urge, opened up the phone's photo gallery and began scrolling through the images. He stopped at one of him and Maggie on a beach on Kauai. He had taken her there as a reward for graduating from law school. Adele had begged off due to some vague work commitment and the length of the flight. Fortunately, her absence provided Luke and Maggie with the infrequent opportunity to catch up and renew their relationship. To his regret, he had been absent more often than not during Maggie's formative years. Still, their relationship had always seemed to weather these interruptions. It remained unclear whether this was due to the transitory impermanence of youth or Maggie's innate resilience.

He flicked through several other images. One of him and Adele on a motorcycle in Scotland. A photo of Adele in dress uniform receiving a citation of some sort, Maggie in cap and gown at her law school graduation, he and Adele on either side of her. Another of the three of them on a hiking trip in the Dolomites. In all of them, there was a suggestion, an impression of happiness, if not contentment. Where it had all fallen apart remained the source of many a late night self-reflection.

He slumped back on the bed, overcome by a sudden fit of despair. The incident at Bardarash had shaken him and made him realize just how precarious all his connections had become. And seeing the young woman's corpse had carved out some part of him, her battered image a familiar visitor to his nightmares. He sat up as if jolted. It did no good to dwell on the past, not now. He turned off the phone, grabbed his jacket and seaman's watch cap and set out to find the eatery that Masoud had pointed out.

12

Five minutes later, he came across a narrow side street and recognized the heavy wooden sign jutting out from above a deeply set doorway. Masoud had provided a rough translation. "The Blood Of My Favorite Ox." He stepped inside and was immediately overwhelmed by the smell of roasting meat, garlic, and some other spice he couldn't place. The small, adobe brick dining room was dimly lit, the majority of the tables occupied by locals gauging from their appearance. A tinny sound system blared out Middle Eastern music. Out of some subconscious and long practiced habit, he took a table in the corner with his back to the wall.

The waitress appeared to be barely pubescent, most likely the daughter of the woman rattling pans in the open kitchen; the squat man behind the counter likely her father. To his surprise, the girl spoke passable English. He ordered dolmas, a lamb stew, flatbread and a bottle of Ava Zêr, a Kurdish beer brewed in the Czech Republic that he had sampled in Erbil. When she returned with his beer, he showed her Maggie's picture on his phone. She simply shook her head no.

The lamb dish reminded him of a similar stew he and Adele had eaten at a small roadside diner near Monument Valley, the most prominent item on the diner's menu Navajo stew. The taste brought back a sudden flood of memories of that trip and starlit desert campsites and bathing in cold streams. At the time, their relationship was still fresh, on the cusp of commitment.

His thoughts were interrupted when a pair of men rode a gust of wind through the front door. They wore rather tattered, soiled hiking pants, muddy boots, and expensive looking, though well worn, shell parkas. Both appeared youngish, thirties maybe, with long hair and unkempt beards. They looked sun baked and might have even passed for locals except for their clothing and bearing. They surely didn't seem to be Kurds or Arabs. They scanned the small dining room and chose the table nearest to Luke. They each nodded to him a greeting and began studying the menu. When the waitress took their order, he caught their accents. One was a Brit for sure, the other sounded as if he was French.

As Luke ate, he watched them out of the corner of his eye and tried to catch snippets of their murmured conversation. They both appeared haggard, their faces slack with exhaustion. The one who seemed British had reddish hair, a long thin face with ears flat to his head, and hooded eyes. His companion's face was soft, almost feminine and his beard displayed at least a crude attempt at grooming. Even from three feet away he could smell their rank body odor. He could tell by the way they downed their beers that they were trying to satisfy a thirst that wasn't necessarily in their throats. He waited until they ordered their second round of beer before leaning over and asking them how well they knew Duhok.

The Brit mumbled though a mouthful of flatbread. "Don't. Actually we just got here. You?" His accent sounded Cockney.

"I just arrived here, too. I'm curious. Do you work for any of the NGOs?'

The Brit looked at his partner briefly before replying. "No. We're journalists. Least ways, Oliver here is. I just take the pictures. We just creeped over from Syria."

"Is that easy to do? To cross the border?"

The Brit shook his head. "Not likely. We'd been pissin' around in this shaggy village waiting for someone to shuttle us across. It's not as easy as it seems."

"Are there still refugee camps on the Syrian side?"

"Sure. Not so many though. None of them are very large. It seems that everyone that could make it already skipped to the camps over here on the Iraqi side. It's not easy over there. A lot of brown bread if you catch my drift. Grim is what I mean." He flashed a toothy, inappropriate grin. "Not much aid coming in to those places. Dangerous, too. Creepin' around Syria, I mean."

Luke turned on his iPhone and searched for the picture of Maggie. "Is there any chance you might've seen this young woman?" He held it out to the Brit who studied for several seconds and shook his head.

"Sorry, can't say I have."

"How about you?" Luke asked, holding the phone out to the other man.

The Frenchman took a long pull of his beer, wiped his hands on his pants and took the phone. He studied it for no more than two or three seconds and nodded. He kept looking at it for a moment longer. "Yes. I am fairly certain I saw her."

"What?" his friend asked. "A twist like her I would've remembered."

"I saw her before you arrived at the village. I saw her twice."

"You're sure?" Luke asked, taking the phone back. "Where? What village?"

"The place is called Tel Sayyid. It is in the hills above the Euphrates. Not far from the border."

"What was she doing there?"

Oliver shrugged. "I was being concealed there by our courier. Waiting for Ian here to show up," he said nodding at the Brit. "You couldn't walk around the village because of informers and the chance of militias. But there was a window from where I could see a neighboring house. I could only see part of it because …a lorry…a truck was parked with its bed against the front of the house. There was someone always sitting there, in front of the truck as if they were…" He pointed at his eye and flicked his finger. "Keeping the eye on things. Isn't that the American expression? The first morning I was there, it was just after dawn, I saw this woman come outside to wash up at the water pump. She was with a man that seemed... he seemed as if he was anxious for them to return inside. He was shouting at her. She was blonde like the photo you showed me." He held a finger in the air, and paused to take a swallow of his beer,

"The next day I saw her again. I saw her face more clearly because she looked directly at me. I stepped away from the window, but I am positive she saw me. It was this woman you showed me. The same. I am very certain of it."

"What was she doing?"

"This second time she seemed angry. She shouted at the man who followed her outside. She kept pointing to the truck and screaming in what I thought at the time might be German and then it sounded like English. I couldn't really hear it that well. After a few minutes, another man came from the house and they dragged her back into the house. I never saw her again. Ian came later that day and we left that very night."

"This was when?"

"Three. No. Four days ago."

"Is there anything else you remember?'

"No. Nothing else."

"How about the men she was with. What did they look like?"

"The men? Young. They might've been Kurds. At least they didn't look to be Arabs. I'm sorry, but that is all I can tell you."

"So who is the girl?" Ian asked.

"Someone I need to find. This village. Tel Sayyid. How would I find it?"

"We arrived there at night," the Frenchman replied. "We were hidden in a truck so I did not see it well. It is on the Syrian side of the Euphrates. We had to cross the river in a dinghy to reach the border which wasn't far."

"Yeah, that fookin' dinghy," Ian added. "Cold crossing that river at night. It might be on a map. Or maybe not. From what I saw the place wasn't very large."

"And the house? What did it look like?"

The Frenchman thought for a moment. "It was built of stone. Like flat stones. Stacked? Yes?" he said, motioning with his hands. "The door was painted blue. And wait, I remember. Behind the house was a water tank. On a wooden platform."

"A water tower?"

"Yes, a water tower. With something in red painted on the side. Something in Arabic."

"Was the village patrolled by the militias?"

"Not that I saw, but it seemed everyone kept hidden inside for most of the day."

Luke sat back and thought for a moment. He couldn't see where he had much choice but to check it out. The description the Frenchman gave surely matched Maggie. How many women like that could there be roaming around in northern Syria? Going there, however, would require some planning and surely more help than Masoud alone could provide. He wished there was a way to contact Masoud tonight, but unfortunately he would have to wait until morning. He paid his bill, and stood to leave.

"Good luck, mate. I hope you find her," Ian said. "A word of advice though. You go rabbitin' around over there you're likely to get your arse in the knockers. Best go with someone who knows his way around."

Luke nodded his thanks and left. Outside, the night had grown colder, the wind stiffer, and he could smell the snow in the air. As he walked back to the hostel, he decided he would try calling Adele.

13

JOHN F. KENNEDY INTERNATIONAL AIRPORT
NEW YORK
NOVEMBER 22ND

Adele hung back and waited behind the throng of her fellow passengers lining up beside the baggage carousel. She glanced up at the screen for the third time to make sure she was at the correct carousel for it seemed to be taking an inordinate amount of time for their bags to arrive. She felt done in, having not slept on the plane, much less the night before back in her apartment in Munich. For a moment, she toyed with the idea of getting a hotel room and catching a few hours of sleep, but there really wasn't sufficient time to be procrastinating. She felt secure in her mind as to what needed to be done. It was how she should proceed that was giving her second thoughts. She checked her watch. 8AM. Sleep would have to wait.

She rubbed her eyes and when she lowered her hand, she became aware of someone standing next to her, close enough to brush shoulders. She gave the person a quick appraisal out of the corner of her eye. It was a man of average height, wearing a raincoat and staring up at the monitor. She picked up her carry-on and moved a few steps closer to the carousel.

"Ms. Marchand."

She turned and looked at the man, but he kept his gaze fixed on the monitor. Upon closer inspection, he appeared to be almost purposefully nondescript, fortyish, thick glasses with heavy black frames, pale complexion, thinning reddish hair, and a nose that seemed to have seen its share of abuse gauging from the thick scar just below the bridge of his glasses. His raincoat looked cheap and rumpled.

"We should talk," he said, lowering his gaze and looking over his shoulder, still not meeting her gaze. "How about that bench over there? The bags will be a while," he said, turning and giving her what looked to be a hint of a smile. He turned and walked to the bench without waiting for her reply.

She could guess what this was about. For some reason, perhaps because of her old job, she was probably on a watch list of some sort. Or was it something else? The phone call last night came quickly to mind. She hesitated a moment before walking over to the bench. She recognized his type, having worked with them enough times. Mid-level desk jockey, she guessed, possibly an ex- field officer now in harness by choice or decree. They all seem to exude a certain aura. Something in their posture perhaps, the way they surveyed their surroundings; a kind of bored vigilance born of groomed habit. The question was which one of a dozen or so intelligence agencies he worked for. She suddenly realized the error of her ways in reaching out last night to her friend at Langley.

"Would it be out of line to see some credentials?" she asked, making no effort to sit.

At first, he didn't reply, but after a moment, he reached into the pocket of his jacket and produced a wallet which he flipped open just long enough for Adele to see the logo and catch the last name. The brief glance allowed her to see the photo roughly resembled the man sitting before her.

"So what can I do for you, Mr. Graham?" She sat down a couple of feet away, placing her carry on between them.

"You look tired," he said. "Too many late night phone calls, maybe? Look," he said when she didn't reply. "I'm aware of your background, so I'll come straight to the point. We'd just like to know the reason for your inquiries about a certain Mr. Ozbek."

She paused to watch a young man turn and glance at her as he passed by. She had noticed him in line at the boarding gate in Munich. She had subconsciously profiled him. Middle Eastern, no carry on, only a book. Nervous, maybe. Or was she simply being paranoid?

"I am not so naïve as to think you don't already know. Okay, maybe you don't know. My daughter was romantically involved with Ozbek. They went to Syria together. She wanted to visit the refugee camps, and he said he was going to visit family in Kurdistan. Satisfied?"

"We know what the BND told you. So you must realize he was lying."

She stared at him for a moment before replying. "Something tells me you are not here to provide me with further information."

"No, I'm afraid I can't add much, at least nothing of substance."

"Can't or won't? So, you're wasting both our time. Perhaps you would be willing to tell me though why the interest in Ozbek."

Graham shrugged. "That's above my pay grade. I was just told to ask what your interest might be and report back. I'm just the conduit of information."

"A one-way conduit."

"You surely understand how these things work. So I tell the powers that be that you're simply trying to find your daughter. Is that it?"

"I am flying to Baghdad tomorrow night, but I am sure you already knew that. I am going to Iraq to find my daughter. The end of story."

"You're going there to find your ex-husband, too. Right?" When she didn't reply, he went on. "Do you know what you're getting into? Going there, I mean."

"I can guess. Tell me. Have you ever been over there?"

"You mean Iraq? Sure. Desert Storm. Fallujah. I was a S2 intelligence analyst. Your file says that's what you did. Why do you ask?"

She started to reply but paused as the luggage carousel started up. "Goodbye, Mr. Graham," she said, getting to her feet.

"The fact remains you called one of our analysts in an unofficial capacity requesting classified information."

"Tell me. Is my friend in trouble?"

"Let's just say he's probably not your friend any longer."

"He didn't disclose anything I didn't already know."

"It makes no difference. You were asking questions about something you had no need to know about."

"Which only makes me more curious why you're interested in a Turkish intelligence agent posing as a Kurd who happens to go into Syria a week before Turkey invades Syria."

Graham cocked his head. "Let me give you some advice. You need to keep your distance from all this. It's for your own good."

"Are you trying to frighten me, Mr. Graham?"

"Something tells me you're not the type that frightens easily. I'm just warning you. Consider it a professional courtesy. All I can tell you is that when you asked about him, some red flags went up. I don't know why. Like I said, it's above my pay grade."

"And what if I happen to stumble across this Ozbek? Should I give him your regards? Shoot up a signal flare?"

Graham didn't reply. She sensed he wanted to tell her something more, but just then his cell phone chimed. He glanced at the message and then nodded at the baggage carousel. "By the way, we checked your bag. You might be interested to know the Iraqis don't always check that closely any more flying into Baghdad."

He rose to his feet and walked off without saying another word. She watched him disappear into the crowd before walking over to the carousel to look for her bag.

"Mein Gott, Maggie. Was hast du getan?" she muttered to herself. She had already grown worried after hearing what the BND knew about Murat. Luke's video message did little to alleviate her concern. And now this. Everything told her that Maggie had stepped into what Luke used to call a shit storm, and obviously a dangerous one at that. All of this only served to harden her resolve.

She spotted her bag, but before taking it, she turned and glanced once more around the claim area. Graham was nowhere to be seen, nor was the young Middle Eastern man. If she allowed herself to give into her paranoia, she could surely spot a half-dozen other suspicious faces. She grabbed her bag and walked out of the terminal.

14

They were driving down a dusty, rutted road. Desert hardpan stretched as far as the eye could see. In the distance, rose dozens of spiraling columns of black smoke. In front of them, drove a large truck, the open flat bed packed with children of various ages. They all appeared gaily dressed and were dancing, their wild gyrations rocking the truck wildly to and fro. Harper became aware that she was sitting alone in the back seat of a luxury sedan of some sort; leather seats, tinted windows, the cold air blowing from the air conditioning venting streams of pinkish vapor. Only then did she notice the two people in the front seat. The passenger, the back of his bald head his only visible feature, roared in laughter. The driver turned to look at him, joining in his laughter. It was Rodavan driving. He lifted his gaze in the rear view mirror to wink at Harper, and then began leaning on the car's horn. It made an odd ringing sound over and over. And that's when she awoke.

She lifted her head and blinked in the bright light of the floor lamp above her head before glancing around the room. Daylight, she guessed by the thin frame of light leaking around the blackout curtains. She struggled to a sitting position, spilling the pile of papers from her chest onto the floor. She heard the ringing again. Through her fog she realized it was her doorbell.

She squinted at her watch. 10 AM. The ringing now came in short, persistent bursts. She lie there another moment before swinging her feet off the sofa and pushing unsteadily to her feet. Grimacing, she shuffled to the door and jammed the intercom button with the heel of her hand. She ran her tongue around her mouth in an attempt to work up enough saliva to be able to say something.

"Yeah," she croaked, finally.

A few seconds passed. "It is Adele," her tinny voice almost drowned out by the sound of a passing truck.

"Adele," Harper murmured, leaning her head against the doorjamb. "What do you want?" she managed to ask after a moment.

"There is something I must show you."

Harper thought for a moment, her head still resting on the door frame. "Okay. Come on up. The door's open," she said, punching the entry button. She unlocked the trio of door locks and turned to survey the living room. Manny's files were strewn on the coffee table and the floor. She scooped up the loose papers and stuffed them back into the manila folder before shoving it under the sofa seat cushion. The wine bottle and the vial of Ritalin tablets should go, too, she decided, scooping them up. She took another quick inventory and headed for her bathroom.

Leaning over the sink, she took note of the damage. Her eyes stared back blearily, her lids puffy. She splashed her face with cold water several times, took a gulp of mouth wash, gargled and spit. Lifting the collar of her sweat shirt over her nose, she took a whiff. All she could smell was the mouthwash. No sense changing clothes anyway, she thought just as she heard the front door open and shut. This was insane, she thought; this collusion with Adele. And now she was here in New York; in her apartment. She took stock in the mirror once more and then strolled out to the living room with as much poise as she could manage to muster.

Adele stood just inside the small foyer, her head swiveling somewhat warily about the apartment.

"Pardon the mess," Harper said, walking over to the picture window and swiping the curtains open. She squinted into the bright morning sunlight and turned and looked at Adele who still hadn't budged. "I'll make coffee.

I hope you take it black. No milk," Harper said, making her way to what passed for her kitchen. Not that she ever used it for more than the basics – coffee and reheating take out.

"Black is fine."

Adele wore a charcoal gray, quilted jacket atop black woolen trousers. She clutched what appeared to be a laptop under her arm. Only then did Harper notice the carryon bag and the larger suitcase next to the door.

"I came directly from JFK," Adele said, noting Harper's gaze.

"Why are you here?" Harper asked, shoveling two handfuls of coffee beans down the throat of the expensive Italian coffee maker her agent had given her as a birthday present. Adele's reply was drowned out by the grinder.

"I said that I needed to show you something," she said after the grinder stopped. "I thought it was important."

Harper turned and saw Adele was leaning over something on the floor. Adele made a grunting sound and then picked something up. Harper could see it was one of the photographs from Manny's file.

Adele looked up from the photo, her face registering confusion. "Where did you get this?"

Harper shrugged, "I didn't ask."

"My compliments to your researcher. Or your cat burglar," Adele said, looking back at the photo. "I remember this. I haven't seen it in years. It was taken at the Frankfurt Zoo. 1996. The happy family," she said, holding it up so Harper could see. "*Einmal*," she muttered. "We were once, all of us, happy."

Harper remembered seeing it. A grinning Luke squatting in front of the giraffe corral, a blonde haired child of perhaps five or so propped on his knee. A younger version of Adele stood behind them. Her smile appeared strained. The child, Maggie, Harper assumed, seemed distracted by something, her gaze settling off to the side. There was no telling how Manny had managed to get hold of a copy of the photo.

Adele glanced at it again and dropped it onto the coffee table before walking over to a wall that displayed a collage of framed photographs. "You have a very nice apartment," she said, absently as she studied the photos.

Harper's apartment, a spacious two bedroom, one bath, walkup held the flotsam of a career spent mostly overseas; Oriental rugs, mismatched teak furniture, exotic knickknacks, carved masks, and photos that covered virtually every available wall space. At one time, before she adopted Funaya, the apartment served as nothing more than a stopover; a place to do her laundry, catch up on emails, and make futile attempts at sleep. Funaya had changed that; tethering her in place. Now, she spent the majority of her time at home so as to be available for Funaya. The recent trip to Kurdistan had been the exception.

Harper poured them each some coffee and set the cups on the coffee table. Picking up the photo, she glanced at it for a second, and tossed it back on the table. "Did you really think I wasn't going to do some research?"

"Did it reveal anything incriminating?" Adele said, plopping down on a chair opposite Harper.

"Why didn't you mention that you worked at your embassy in Prague?"

Adele shrugged. "I thought it without relevance. Besides, I don't work there anymore. Your information is outdated. All I did there was to ensure the Czechs imported enough BMWs, and we imported our share of porcelain knick knacks and pharmaceuticals. Is that the sum of my deceptions?"

"So far. How about Armstrong Technics?"

"They are a client. I do vetting of their potential hires."

Neither of them said anything for a moment as they both sat sipping their coffee.

"You said you had something to show me."

Adele picked up the laptop from the floor beside her chair and opened it. "I downloaded this from my iPhone. Luke sent it yesterday." She powered up the laptop, tapped a few keys and then set it on the table and spun it around for Harper to see. "It is not a very good transmission. I have someone seeing if it can be cleaned up, but he is not optimistic."

The screen abruptly revealed Luke's face filling the usual oblong-shaped cell phone screen. He was leaning close in, and one could easily see his red-rimmed eyes and unshaven face. Even though the lighting was poor, one could see he looked more than just haggard; defeated maybe.

"... hope you get this," he said, his voice raspy. "...says two bars, but not... I tried..."

The call kept dropping, the video image distorted. There was a burst of static lasting for what seemed almost ten seconds.

"...came to Duhok to..." Again the static. "...try tomorrow....ask around. I went to Bardarash, but couldn't..." The visual and the sound disappeared in a blitz of static before resuming. "...this French guy thinks he saw her, but it's going to be ..." The static again, something garbled "... a village in Syria....likely dangerous to..."

He disappeared again for several seconds. When the signal returned, Luke had leaned away from the phone, "... if text doesn't go...try email. ... worry. I'll call..." And then the screen went blank.

Neither of them said anything for a moment. "I tried calling him back. I left a message, but so far he has not tried back. No email either," Adele said, closing the laptop.

"Too bad it wasn't a better connection. So what did you make out of what he said?"

"I am not sure. It sounds like he went to one of the camps. Bardarash. It sounded like maybe someone might have seen her there. And he was going back to check it out. I had to listen to it a half dozen times. I was an intelligence analyst, but still I find I am often only guessing at things. I do know he was calling from Duhok. The friend who is trying to clean up the

transmission was able to provide a GPS location from where the call originated. That is a start, I guess."

"Did I hear right something about checking out some village in Syria?
And something about it maybe being dangerous. Jesus, Adele, do you even
know where Maggie was going?"

"I told you. She called two weeks or so after the invasion. From
Al-Qamishli. She and... this Murat, they..." She shook her head in what
seemed annoyance. "Something wasn't right. I could tell from her voice."

"You said she wanted to see some of the camps. But what about this
Murat guy? You know he's Turkish, right?"

Adele shot her a quick, hard look. "How did you know that?"

"My home work."

Adele fell silent as if she were carefully considering what to say. "Yes,
he is Turkish. He said he was a Kurd, which turned out to be a lie. One of
his many deceptions."

"What do you mean?"

Adele started to say something before hesitating and starting over.
"Maggie told me once that he was a deserter from the Turkish Army and
was hiding out in Germany. At first, I took her at her word. I assumed she
knew him well enough. I let it go." She hesitated again as if she were editing
in her mind what to say next. "But after they left, I was able to find out that
he flew out of Berlin using a Turkish passport, but using a different name."

Harper nodded. "And you were going to tell me this when?"

"I found this..." She started over. "I just found all this out yesterday.
Before then, all I knew was what he told me, that he was going into Kurdistan
to see his brother. A family reunion of some sort. This was still before the
invasion when the Kurdish region of Syria was relatively quiet. Not much
fighting. ISIS was gone. I thought..." Her voice drifted off.

"And?"

Adele slumped back in her chair and clasped her hands over her mouth, her eyes registering despair. "Very well," she said finally. "I contacted a former colleague, Someone who has access to many things."

"You mean someone in the intelligence field."

Adele nodded. She raised he coffee cup to her mouth but then seemed to change her mind. "Yes. The BND if you must know. The German equivalent of your CIA. I told you. I still have contacts there. It turns out Murat isn't his real name. And he is not a Kurd either. His real name is Emin Ozbek. They are quite certain he is a Turkish intelligence agent stationed in Berlin. He isn't…wasn't…"

Adele lowered her head into her hands. "*Gott verdammt!*" She looked away and swiped at her eyes. "Maggie…she was taken in by this man. I was taken in by this man. She allowed herself to be duped into going with him into Syria. Just as I was duped! *Dieser verdammt Turk!*" she shrieked. "*Der Giftzwerg!*"

Harper started to reach for Adele's hand but she pulled away.

"It only gets worse," Adele said calmly, her fury spent. "The German Federal Police consider him a possible suspect in the murders of two Turkish students in Berlin last summer. Dissidents that the Turkish government was trying to silence. I found out he was also on the BND's watch list."

"If he's Turkish intelligence than why is he sneaking into Syria? Pre-invasion intelligence gathering? I guess that's possible. Right?"

"Or perhaps sabotage. But why take Maggie along? All I can think is that Maggie was accompanying him to provide some sort of cover to help get him across the border. Or maybe into the camps? But to what purpose?"

She stood and walked over to the window. After a moment, she turned and looked at Harper. "I have already booked a flight to Baghdad that leaves tomorrow night. From there I will make my way to Erbil. There are no connecting flights to Erbil for at least two days. I'll have to take a bus or hire someone to take me there. Baghdad must have Uber," she added with a smile,

"You're crazy."

"Once I get to Erbil, it appears it is not that far to this Bardarash camp."

"Have you thought this all out? You're going to need a visa."

"I already have one."

"Don't tell me, Your contacts?"

Adele shrugged.

"Okay, You're going to need more than a visa."

"I thought you said you could arrange some press credentials I might use."

"Sure. I can probably arrange that. You're supposed to get a journalist's permit in Baghdad, but with a visa, the press credentials, and a bribe you can manage. Just be careful not to flash too much money around."

"I know that."

"Of course, you do," Harper said with a hint of sarcasm. "Still, if you travel on your own…"

"I have to keep believing that if she is there, Luke will find her. But he might need help. I'll find him first. If I don't find out anything at the camp, then I will go to Duhok and check out the hostel he called from. Hopefully by then I would've heard from him. I emailed him about what I found out about this Ozbek. As I said, he hasn't replied. Perhaps… " She shrugged, clearly frustrated.

"I would assume he's already gotten some help. But as for you, you can't just waltz in there on your own."

"It almost sounds as if you are offering."

"I didn't say that. It's just…" Harper thought back to what Funaya had told her. That she needed to help find someone's missing daughter; an adopted daughter, no less. It is only right, Funaya had said.

"I told you once before I might be able to help you find a fixer. There's someone in Mosul I used once before. He can find us…" She quickly corrected herself. "He can find you a driver and a translator in Erbil, probably some security as well. They should be able to get you to Bardarash."

"Perhaps, I should go to Duhok first."

"And what? Go door to door by yourself looking for Luke?"

"You could help me."

"I already said I could get you credentials and arrange for a driver. That should be help enough."

Adele came back and sat in the chair. "Very well. I will go to the camp first. Look, all I ask is that you go with me at least as far as Bardarash. Just get me into the camp."

"You're right about it not being far from Erbil. I've been there. It's run by the UNHCR. It had quite a few refugees when I was there, mostly Syrian Kurds. It has to be a lot larger since the invasion." Harper met Adele's gaze. "You don't know what you're asking."

Harper lifted her eyes to stare at the wall above Adele's head at a photograph of Funaya and her taken at a school social event. She thought for a moment and then slumped back in resignation. "Okay. I'll go with you to Bardarash, but that's as far as I go."

But there's no way I'm going to Duhok, she told herself. Not if there was any chance Luke might be there. It wasn't the time or place for a reunion; not under these circumstances. Her awkwardness with Adele was the other half of her reluctance. So why was she agreeing to come along? Maybe it was just simple curiosity. She assumed everyone had someone in their past that they would like to just run across. And catch up with. Divulge your secrets. Or not. Yes, she was curious. She was paid to be curious. In simple terms, it's what she did.

"I checked this morning," Adele said, interrupting her thoughts. "There are still seats left on the flight to Baghdad."

"Why do I feel like I've been played?"

"I know what I am asking, Harper. And I am grateful. I know that may not be enough."

"You're right. Nothing's ever enough," she muttered under her breath. She stood and went back into the kitchen and poured herself another cup of coffee. "My visa's still good. I'll get to work on your credentials. Iraq will be cold up north this time of year. Are you packed for that?"

"Maybe I should do some shopping."

"There's an REI about four blocks from here on Lafayette. And while you're out, pick us up some food. And maybe some wine. And while you're at it, a bottle of Hendricks."

Adele slipped on her raincoat, started for the door and then turned. "I must know something. Why are you going? Is it because of Luke? Or are you perhaps just chasing a story?"

"I don't know, maybe a little of both. I should ask you why you're so determined I go with you."

"Maybe the same reason this Ozbek took Maggie with him. You will be my cover. We will be two journalists. The truth is I don't know anyone else that knows that country. Or more importantly, someone who might care enough about my daughter. Someone who understands what a mother would do for their child." She shook her head and smiled. "Maggie was a difficult child. Headstrong, poor regulation skills. And reckless. But she's smart and tough. I will find her. I'll find both of them," she said in a way that came off sounding less than convincing.

Harper nodded. "I need to take a hot bath and ask myself some serious questions," she said and started to go into the bathroom before hesitating. She waited until Adele left before finding her cell phone and dialing the number.

"Hey Manny. It's me. You said you might know someone who could do some deeper checking. Yeah? I want him to look into a Turkish guy named Emin Ozbek." She spelled it for him. "To make it more interesting for your friend, tell him this Ozbek is a Turkish intelligence agent. Yeah, like a spy.

And tell him to feel free to hack into Turkish military intelligence. Sure I'm serious. For god sakes, tell him they do that in the movies all the time," she said, laughing. "Let him know I'd make it worth the risk. Use my email because I'll be on the road. Yeah, I know. *Muy estupido.* I owe you." She eyed the bottle of wine on the kitchen counter, but then thought better of it and retreated to the bathroom.

PART THREE

"Only the dead have seen the end of war"
-Plato

15

ERBIL, IRAQ
KURDISH AUTONOMOUS REGION
NOVEMBER 24TH

The Fiori Hotel was a half-star shy of five and presumably a bargain at two hundred and fifty dollars a night. Adele was glad she had pawned her wedding ring at a shop in the diamond district before leaving New York. She surely didn't feel comfortable carrying around a belt bag containing twenty something thousand dollars, not in Iraq, not anywhere, no matter how nice the hotel seemed. But experience told her that she might need a lot of cash to find Maggie. The question was whether simply finding her would be the sum total of it. She somehow doubted it, and that likelihood depressed her to no end. So far, she had resolutely avoided considering any dire outcomes, regardless of how much time had lapsed.

She rattled the ice cubes in her glass in an attempt to get the bartender's attention and pointed at her glass. She glanced at her watch again. Eleven PM Iraqi time. Six AM New York time. Munich? She should be drinking coffee, not vodka. That or be in her room sleeping like Harper. Their flight to Baghdad had taken twenty-one hours, including a five-hour layover in Istanbul. It had taken another hour to clear customs in Baghdad, and then a five hour, relatively uneventful drive to Erbil. And here she was, not even unpacked, and shutting the place down.

Actually, she was casting bait. The incident at JFK with Graham only reinforced her suspicion that there was a great deal more to Ozbek than she had been led to believe. Why else their reaction to her informal inquiry? Her experience and instincts told her she was being watched.

Standard operating procedure would mean placing someone on the plane, if not in New York, then surely at the stopover in Istanbul. At the least, someone would have taken up their trail at baggage claim in Baghdad. For that matter, she might be under surveillance at this very moment.

She turned in her chair and glanced around the bar. There was only one other customer sitting by himself in the corner seemingly absorbed in his laptop. Thirty something, shaved head, olive complexion. He looked local enough to blend in, she thought turning back to the bar. She couldn't be certain whether she had noticed him before.

Ever since 911, her intelligence analyst background had kicked into over drive. Whenever she flew, she surreptitiously scanned the faces of everyone boarding, mentally profiling them. This paranoia only exacerbated her inherent anxiety. The man is the booth was most likely just a businessman, she decided after several moments more of consideration.

She tried again to resolve her guilt over deceiving Harper. That night in Ljubljana was when she should have revealed more than merely her reservations about Maggie's plans. She should have told Harper then what she knew about Ozbek, but that would have surely dissuaded Harper from becoming involved. It was the same reason she had held back telling Harper about her call to the friend at Langley and the subsequent encounter with Graham. She needed Harper.

Initially, she had approached Harper for no other reason than to acquire press credentials and her contacts. Asking Harper to accompany her had been an impulse, and perhaps a foolish one. But as things played out, she realized Harper might prove useful, if for no other reason than to provide a buffer between her and Luke.

At some point, Harper would probably grow suspicious and realize that all was not as it seemed. The subject of her intelligence contacts had already been raised. She couldn't be sure if Harper had believed her or not. She wouldn't blame Harper if she didn't buy her explanation.

Those deceptions aside, what Adele found even more mortifying was the prospect of having to confess to Harper just how negligent she had been in not vetting Ozbek the moment Maggie had introduced him to her. Any mother would've asked questions. That is what mothers do, isn't it? Yet here she was, an intelligence analyst for god sakes, and she hadn't asked questions, hadn't done the necessary research that would've prevented all this from happening in the first place.

Harper would have to find out everything at some point, just not yet, she decided just as the bartender, a stocky young Kurd sporting a shoulder length pony tail, delicately placed another drink in front of her and bowed his head. She rewarded him with a smile. Fortunately, the Kurds, unlike their Arab brethren in the south of Iraq, had little regard for prohibitions on the sale or consumption of alcohol. Nor did they expect large gratuities.

She downed most of her vodka and tonic and opened up her phone. There was still no email or text from Luke. Where could he be that he hadn't responded? He needed to know about Ozbek. She felt uncomfortable imparting all she knew in an email or a text. It was her paranoia again; that or too many years listening into other people's phone conversations.

The possibility of something having happened to Luke only heightened her anxiety. It was likely that Luke was merely somewhere without any cell reception. Or was he just being true to form and was too bull-headed to reply? Her anxiety was giving way to annoyance. She put away her phone and downed the rest of her vodka just as Harper slid into the stool next to her.

"Too wired to rest," Harper explained.

Adele hoisted her drink. Harper shook her head.

"I better not. Actually, I came down to give you an update. The driver my guy in Mosul was arranging for us was in a traffic accident. He won't be able to get another vehicle for maybe two days."

"I don't have two days to wait."

"I realize that. He said driving to Duhok though shouldn't be a problem. There'll most likely be a checkpoint or two, but we should be able to get through. We have papers and our visas. I suppose we can see if the hotel can arrange a car and at the least a driver."

"Suppose we just rent a car and drive ourselves?"

"Jesus. Adele. Have you listened to anything I've told you?"

"Just to Duhok. I already checked. It is not far. The roads should be fine. Like you said, we shouldn't have any problem."

"I don't care. We should have a guardian angel. You don't know what you'll run into."

"Are you trying to make me more anxious than I already am?"

"You've seemed pretty calm so far. Inappropriately calm in fact."

Adele hoisted her glass again. "Two vodkas and twenty milligrams of Lorazepam. It is a wonder I am still awake. Do you see the man sitting in that booth?" she asked, tilting her head. "Tell me. Did you happen to see him at the airport?"

Harper took a quick glance over her shoulder. "No. Why?"

"Just curious."

"I think I'll change my mind on that drink," she said, pointing at Adele's glass after getting the bartender's attention. "Do you want another?"

"*Nein.* I have had plenty. *Zu viel,*" Adele added, fishing the last pistachio out of the bowl at her elbow. "Let me ask you. Have you ever been married?"

"Once. It didn't take and I never tried it again. I figured my career wasn't conducive to long term commitments."

"But you've had your share of lovers?"

"Where's this coming from? Is it just the booze or are you still curious about Luke and me?"

"I told you I knew all about Sarajevo. I would be lying if I told you I haven't wondered what would've happened if... you know..."

Harper paused as the bartender set her drink in front of her. "You mean what would've happened if I hadn't been raped and beaten half to death? Or if I had..." She seemed to stop herself from saying more. "You need to ask Luke," she said after a moment. "fter he got me to the hospital in Italy I never heard from again. I'd be lying if I said I didn't wonder why. I mean there was nothing. No phone call. No letter. Nothing. I don't know if he just felt guilty or what."

Adele stared at her drink for a long moment. "*Schuld, Immer so viel Schuld.,*" she muttered.

"English, please."

"Guilt. There is always so much guilt."

"So now I'm curious. Why did you and Luke break up? Was it another woman?"

"That seems a strange question coming from you."

"You're right. I'm out of line."

Adele's offered a brief smile. "No, it was never because of another woman. Not this time. It was because..." She shrugged. "If you did your homework, you might have found out why he and the Army parted ways. They forced him out, even though he will say he chose to leave. It was all because of an investigation he wanted no part of."

"What kind of investigation?"

"You might as well know. During his last tour in Iraq, he was a Brigade commander. Some of his men were accused of killing a group of innocent women and children in a raid on a house where some anti-government insurrectionist was supposedly hiding. One of the soldiers being court-martialed testified that Luke had specifically sent them to the house to kill this man and everybody else hiding there. He said Luke had even personally inspected the house afterwards and congratulated them for killing ten women and five children. It was all a lie, of course. Luke did inspect the house afterwards, and what he saw I believe has haunted him ever since. It soured him on the war, the Army. And the investigation tarnished whatever was left."

"Knowing how much Luke loved the Army, it must've been hard for him."

"Retiring under those circumstances did not suit him well. All that free time gave him too much time to think about things, our marriage for one. He became restless to the point of mania. Never slept, would be out on his motorcycle at all hours. Sometimes he would be gone for days, a week. After a while, he became a ghost."

She gave a wistful shrug of her shoulders. "I sensed he was no longer interested in me. As a woman. But I knew it wasn't because there was someone else. I thought finally that I had perhaps just aged out. That I was no longer attractive. That is nothing that a woman accepts easily. No? Affection can be such a passing thing. When that is gone and you are no longer friends, then…" She shook her head in a way that telegraphed acceptance.

She eyed Harper's drink before going on. "I must be clear and say it wasn't only him. It seemed like one morning I woke up and I failed to recognize the man in the bed next to me. People change and they forget to tell each other."

She started to raise her hand to the bartender but then thought better. "And then one day it was just over. I told you in Ljubljana that I still love him. At least that part is true even if our marriage wasn't. There is something else I should tell you." She hesitated, unsure of herself. "I also was raped. I was only eighteen. I had been drinking in a bar. I stepped outside for some fresh air. These two men followed me outside. I never revealed this to Luke. You would think we would have shared that, especially after what happened to you in Sarajevo. You should know that he felt immense guilt over that. You must realize he is the kind of person that suffers guilt quite easily, almost wantonly. It was how he was raised. As I said, so much guilt."

"He had no reason to feel guilty."

"No? To his mind, he wasn't there to protect you. The ever gallant soldier. Let me ask you. He told me once that it was you who wanted the affair to end. Is that true?"

"Probably. I never had any luck with those kinds of relationships. I knew Luke and I would never amount to anything. Lots of kindling and no logs."

Adele nodded and smiled. "*Keine mehr Schluchzergeschichten.* No more sob stories, okay? So, you will come with me to Duhok? I understand why you feel you have done enough, but you must understand why I have to go. If there is any chance Luke might be there. I must find him."

Harper smiled. "You read that New Yorker profile about me. Then you must know how difficult it is for me to say no to a story."

"A story? That is the only reason you would go?" Adele sucked her ice cubes and looked at Harper and laughed.

"What?'

"I was just thinking how surprised Luke will be when he sees you."

"Yeah, there's that. You know that photograph you saw back in Ljubljana?" Harper asked after a moment. "The one where Luke's confronting that Serbian militiaman? Trying to save that young Bosnian. That was taken on the day he and I first met. I thought I had never seen anyone so brave. You said it. He was ever the gallant soldier. He was all alone out there without backup. This other journalist and I just happened to drive by and saw it happening. The week before the Serbs had killed a couple of UN observers who were doing pretty much the same thing. I asked him later if he felt safe because we were there witnessing it. He said no. He said he was just showing off for me," she said, shaking her head in amusement.

"That sounds like him."

Neither of them said anything for a long moment. "I'm like you," Harper said finally. "I have to think he'll be alright. You'll find Luke. He'll find Maggie, and we can all go home."

"I hope you are right. Now I must get some sleep. Tomorrow, we will arrange for a car. I will buy one if necessary. We are two bold and capable women without need of bodyguards. *Ja?*" She took Harper's hand. "Thank you for coming. I sincerely mean that."

"I just hope I don't regret it," Harper said, finishing her drink. "Now let's get out of this bar."

16

They rose early to arrange for a car and driver with the hotel concierge. It could not be done on such short notice, the concierge assured them. Possibly tomorrow was all he could promise. Harper held her tongue as Adele offered him a sheaf of US dollars for a more vigorous effort. He rather reluctantly directed them to a car rental agency a short walk from the hotel.

The morning, while bright and cloudless, was raw and cold, the wind gusts occasionally forcing one to turn ones face to avoid the flying dust. There were very few buildings on the street higher than two stories, thus providing an unobstructed view of the snow covered mountains to the north. Despite the cold, it felt good to walk after the long flight and a fitful night in the hotel. Harper's monkey mind, fueled by fatigue, vodka, and Ritalin half-life, had played out the various scenarios. The dire possibilities that became paramount at 3AM only made sleep even more difficult. Of course, Luke appeared in all of them as the proverbial wild card.

By dawn, she had pretty much come to the realization that this was by far one of the most harebrained and ill-advised things she had ever under-taken. More than a few of her adventures, as Funaya liked to call them, turned out to be disastrous, if not downright dangerous. But at least she had recognized and accepted the risks ahead of time. With this, she felt like she was blindly navigating into uncharted territory. After her first cup of coffee, she had half-convinced herself into believing there was the possibility of a story here. After her second cup of coffee, her anthem had changed to 'if she couldn't find a story, she would damn well make one'.

Sunlight Auto Rental was housed in a modern looking but grimy, glass-enclosed structure that resembled more an auto showroom than a rental agency. Inside the sunny showroom sat two vehicles: a slightly used -looking Mercedes sedan and a Land Cruiser that appeared to have just left the assembly line. Behind the only desk, sat a young woman dressed in what resembled a flight attendant's uniform, the impression complete down to the snappy scarf and snug tailoring. All that was missing were some little wings on the badge that offered up the name Aska.

"We would like to arrange for a vehicle and a driver," Adele said.

Aska smiled. "For today?"

"Yes, today."

"I am sorry, madam. But that cannot be done on such short notice."

"All of the rental car drivers must be at a convention," Harper quipped, hoping to lighten what she could see was Adele's growing impatience.

"Very well. We don't require a driver. Just rent us a vehicle."

"You wish to sightsee?"

She had large, liquid eyes that forgave her rather abundant eyebrows. Her face was the kind that changed from plain to attractive depending on the tilt of her head.

"We are going to Duhok."

"Oh, yes? Much like Erbil, there is much to see there."

"Do you go there often?" Harper asked.

"Yes, many times to visit my grandmother."

"It's an easy drive?"

Aska shrugged. "Yes, it is not often difficult. Sometimes there is the weather, sometimes the road. Checkpoints," she added, her smile never wavering.

"You will rent us a car?" Adele asked, her growing testiness becoming obvious.

Aska, still smiling broadly, nodded almost too eagerly. "I will require passports, visas, and driver's license. And a credit card, of course."

They each handed her their documents which she then diligently examined. She paused and looked at Harper. "You were just in our country, Miss Harris," she said, making the S sound like a Z.

Harper nodded.

"Welcome back. Your visa says you are a journalist," she said as she started to enter something on her keyboard. "My brother, he was once a journalist," she said, meeting Harper's eyes for a second before resuming her data entry.

"Really? Who does... or did he work for?"

"Freelance, I believe is the word you use," she said, tapping away. "He was killed a little over a year ago. The Daesh ambushed his car. ISIS, yes?"

"I'm sorry," Harper said, glancing at Adele who didn't seem the least bit deflated by Aska's comment.

"I give you free upgrade. The price includes all insurance. Toyota Land Cruiser. Yes?"

"I would like it for one week."

"A week?" Harper said, glancing at Adele.

Adele nodded. Aska gave her the rental agreement and scrawled an X everywhere Adele was expected to sign. Aska then reached into a drawer and retrieved a set of keys and what looked like a map.

"Can you tell us the best way to get there?" Harper asked.

"Certainly," she replied, unfolding the map. "There are two ways, Highway 2 which takes you to Mosul, From there you will continue north on the same highway to Duhok."

"How long is the drive?"

"Two hours, perhaps more. It depends on traffic and checkpoints. There will be a check point just outside of Mosul, and then again before you cross from Iraq into Duhok province. If they are manned by Iraqi Army, there is never a problem. You show them your papers, and that is usually sufficient. Sometimes, there may be Shia militia. But that is usually only at night."

"And there's another way?" Harper asked.

"Yes, it is perhaps a little longer because the road is not always so good." She picked up a highlighter. "Just before you cross into Iraq... Ninawá Province," she said, correcting herself, "You will take this secondary highway north." She traced the road with the highlighter. "To Dara Shakran. Then you go west to the border crossing at Chammah. It is very near. There will be a Peshmerga check point. The Kurdish Army. You understand? They will just wave you through, and then you will encounter Iraqi National Police checkpoint, It is very small, It is never a problem. Then you will see signs to Duhok. The chances are you will encounter only one more check point outside of Duhok. Again Peshmerga. But it is different at night. The militias. The road is very scenic," she added."There are many small villages and views of the mountains."

"Is it safe?"

"Yes. I have never had a problem."

"Then we take the scenic route," Adele said. "If we leave now, we can make it in time for lunch."

Aska handed them back their documents, and still displaying her smile, gestured for them to follow her outside. She led them to a Land Cruiser which wasn't nearly as pristine as the one in the showroom, but still appeared more than serviceable.

"I will drive," Adele said, taking the keys from Aska and opening the driver side door.

Harper shrugged and walked around to the passenger side. Adele stood with the door open and glanced both ways down the almost deserted street.

"That way," Aska said, pointing in the direction behind them. "In two kilometers you will see the sign to Mosul."

Adele slid into the driver's seat, turned on the ignition, and turned the car around and headed off. Harper opened the map and began perusing it. After driving only a couple of blocks, Adele pulled over to the side of the road in front of a small market.

"I will be right back. I want to get us some water," she said and disappeared inside the market.

Harper studied the map for a moment. When Adele didn't return in almost ten minutes, she folded the map and leaned over to look at the market. She could see Adele standing just inside the glassed in front of the market. She appeared to be studying a rack of postcards, but Harper could tell that she seemed more interested by something on the street behind them. Harper turned and looked and saw nothing unusual; cars and buses passing by, several cars and pickups parked alongside the street, a few pedestrians. What was she looking at?

A moment later, Adele returned, carrying a small shopping bag.

"Is everything okay?" Harper asked.

"Of course." She reached into the bag and retrieved a couple of apples and handed one to Harper. "So we are off." She bit into the apple, and holding it in her mouth, started the ignition and swung the SUV out into the roadway.

17

The border crossing at Chammah was much as Aska had described it. The Erbil side was manned only by a pair of Kurdish Army soldiers dressed in neatly pressed camouflage fatigues and armed only with holstered handguns. They did little more than glance at them before waving them through. Obviously, once they left Erbil province they were no longer a Kurdish problem.

Fifty or so yards further down the two lane, poorly paved road was a corridor formed by crumbling concrete barriers, at the end of which was a candy-striped metal barrier. Three soldiers dressed in crisp blue camouflage and red berets waved them down. Only one of them appeared armed with a generic assault rifle. Adele came to a stop and rolled down the window.

The guards appeared to take note of the SUV's license plate, one of them jotting down the plate number in a note pad as his partners approached the Land Cruiser at an almost leisurely pace. He leaned over and peered at them before glancing in the back seat. Harper recognized his shoulder patch as belonging to the Iraqi National Police.

"*Almakan?*" he asked. "Destination," he added when Adele didn't respond.

"Duhok."

"Your papers, please."

Adele handed him everything which he examined carefully before gesturing that he wanted Harper's papers also. He scrutinized them with the same diligence before leaning down to give them the once over.

"Journalists?"

They both nodded, He thought this over before walking over and conferring with one of his colleagues.

"If he asks for our permits, just slip him a fifty," Harper said. "That's all they ever want."

As they waited, Adele adjusted the rear view mirror and seemed to be scanning the road behind them.

"Are you worried we're being followed?" Harper asked. "You keep looking back at something. It seems like very since leaving Erbil your eyes are always looking in the mirror."

"In Germany, we consider that the sign of an elderly driver or an extremely cautious driver. I am both." She shot Harper a grin.

"How about back at the market in Erbil? I could tell you weren't looking at any postcards."

"So? You said yourself one can't be too careful. I am simply being cautious."

"Cautious or paranoid?"

The policeman came back, and just as Harper predicted, asked them for their permits. Without the slightest pretense of guile, Adele reached into her shirt pocket and handed him a folded fifty dollar bill. The policeman slipped the bill into his pocket without comment and handed them back their papers. He flicked them a two-fingered salute and waved to his companion to lift the barrier.

They drove slowly past a line of food stalls lining either side of the road. Adele was forced to come to a halt as a gaggle of bedraggled children mobbed their SUV hawking packages of candy and gum along with plastic bottles containing some vile-looking, florescent green liquid. Harper thought of how often she had encountered this same scene in an array of Third World countries. The children almost looked as they could be interchangeable.

The sight of a young girl sitting beside the roadway and cradling a rag doll prompted Harper to retrieve her camera from her day pack. She took a couple of quick shots, and only then noticed what appeared to be an abandoned gas station just beyond the line of food stalls. Parked beneath the sagging overhang was a dusty, tan-colored Toyota HiLux pickup truck. Leaning against it were three young men dressed in jeans and fatigue jackets. All wore some kind of headband. They seemed to take more than just a casual notice of the SUV as one of the men pointed at them and nudged his companion.

Adele revved the engine and honked the horn, scattering the children. As they drove off, Harper glanced back at the men standing by the HiLux. They seemed to be watching their departure with avid interest. Harper suddenly regretted not arranging for a bodyguard. Was she simply being paranoid, or just giving into a vigilance honed by years of traveling through counties where one's safety was never taken for granted?

A short way down the road was a sign announcing Bardarash 15Km. Adele slowed briefly before continuing on. "Maybe tomorrow," she said, accelerating as if she might change her mind.

They drove for a while through countryside of small farms and olive groves. The few villages they passed appeared only lightly populated. Several of them showed evidence of relatively recent damage, the nature of which Harper could assume was the result of the war. The half-collapsed walls and piles of rubble were again something she had seen too many times before. The road, at times heavily pot-holed, showed little evidence of any routine maintenance. Occasionally, stretches were nothing more than poorly compacted macadam with no shoulders to speak of.

Even with the absence of any traffic, Harper caught Adele compulsively checking both rear view mirrors. After perhaps twenty minutes of this, Harper craned her neck to check the road behind them.

"Do you see them?" Adele asked. "I think I see their dust back on that gravel section."

Sure enough there was a rooster tail of dust a mile or so behind them.

"Well, I doubt we're the only ones driving to Duhok," Harper replied. She tried not to think of the HiLux. "Do you think we're being followed? I didn't see anyone waiting in line behind us at the check point."

"I suspect it is those men in the truck. You saw them, too. What do you think? Are they militia or just… troublemakers?" Adele asked, glancing at Harper.

Harper didn't reply. They drove for another minute or so in silence as Adele continued to flick her eyes at the mirror. The terrain had begun to gain elevation, the roadway lined on either side by deep gullies that gave way to arid looking hardpan hemmed by low flinty hills. They could see to the northwest where the foothills rose in elevation, and beyond that, snow-capped mountains. A sign indicated another 40 Km to Duhok.

"Now they come faster," Adele said, speeding up herself. "I think they are troublemakers. *Räuber vielleicht,*" she muttered. "*Banditen.*"

Harper looked back. They were probably less than a quarter mile behind them. From what she can tell it was the tan HiLux.

"Don't say I didn't warn you," Harper said, turning back. "Do you really think you can outrun them?"

"Probably not."

"So what do we do?"

Adele checked the mirror again. "Do you agree we shouldn't stop?"

"Sure, but if we don't, they'll probably try to run us off the road."

"No doubt," Adele said, easing off on the accelerator.

"What are you doing?"

"I wish to get a better look at them."

Harper looked back. The HiLux was now no more than twenty or thirty yards behind them. Adele suddenly slowed and the Toyota almost rear ended them. Harper could see their faces now. There appeared to be three of them. The one on the passenger side was gesticulating wildly to the driver. Adele edged the Land Cruiser to the right shoulder of the roadway as if inviting them to pass. Sure enough, the HiLux pulled into the left hand lane abreast of them. Adele looked straight ahead, ignoring them. Harper glanced at them out of the corner of their eye. The one on the passenger side was gesturing for them to pull over.

"*Fick dich,*" Adele said calmly, and then jerked the steering wheel sharply to the left.

They obviously hadn't expected this, and the driver overreacted as he swerved to his left. His tires slipped over the edge of the steep shoulder. As he tried to correct back onto the asphalt, the HiLux's front wheel gave way into the soft dirt that sloped down into a deep gulley. The HiLux disappeared into a cloud of dust.

Adele glanced at her mirror. "Do you see them?"

Harper waited for the dust to dissipate. She couldn't see them at first, but then she made out the silhouette of the truck as it tried to climb out of the ditch and back onto the roadway. It failed, sliding back into the ditch. And then again, but on the third attempt it seemed to gain purchase and climb back onto the road.

"We're so screwed," Harper said.

"Would you please give me my handbag from behind the seat?" Adele asked calmly.

The handbag looked the size of a bowling bag and weighed nearly as much. Adele propped the bag on the floor between her feet, and then floored the Land Cruiser, buying them perhaps a mile. Just ahead was what looked to be a small village consisting of a huddle of no more than a dozen or so adobe and stone structures. The road narrowed as it entered the village, its width no more than eight or ten feet at the widest. Just at the far edge of the village, the road appeared to make a sudden dog leg to the right and then straightened before feeding into a steep decline that obscured the road ahead. Adele slammed on the brakes, shifted into reverse, and backed the SUV close alongside the last house.

"What are you doing?" Harper asked. "They're bound to be right behind us."

"We must cripple them." She rolled down their windows. "Do you hear them coming? Tell me when you do."

Harper shook her head in disbelief and leaned her head out the window and listened. The sound of the oncoming truck was faint, and then suddenly louder as it entered the village's narrow street. "They're here."

Adele slipped into gear and nosed the SUV closer to street and revved the engine.

"Seatbelt," she said sternly to Harper as if she were admonishing a recalcitrant child.

It happened quickly, the span of time surely no more than three or four seconds. Adele timed the HiLux's approach perfectly, stomping on the accelerator and popping the clutch just as the truck's front end emerged from the last house. The front of the heavier Land Cruiser smashed into the HiLux's rear quarter panel, spinning it sideways.

Due to the larger Land Cruiser's bulk and the fact it came equipped with a sturdy steel reinforced grill, meant the HiLux's one rear wheel and the pickup's bed were caved in. Adele quickly shifted into reverse, twisted the steering wheel and accelerated, fishtailing back onto the roadway.

Harper looked back in time to see one of the men climb from the HiLux's cab. He raised something that Harper realized was a rifle at the same moment the rear window exploded.

"Hold on," Adele yelled as they careened around a curve, barely missing a pair of sheep grazing next to the road.

Harper twisted around to see if the HiLux had managed to follow them, but saw nothing. After a mile or so, she turned and looked at Adele, whose only sign of discomfiture was a bead of sweat on her upper lip. She turned to Harper and smiled.

"Das war veile Spass? Fun, yes?"

"You crazy fucking Kraut!" Harper yelled, trying to catch her breath. It was only then she noticed that the passenger side window had also been blown out by the bullet. "That could've gone very wrong."

"Yes. *Aber alles vorbei.* We are okay now," she said, mashing the accelerator with Teutonic zeal.

Harper kept glancing behind them, but the road remained clear.

"Before our next brush with death, tell me the truth. Is there any chance you're bipolar?"

Adele's mouth curled into a pantomime of a grin. "Bipolar? Whatever would give you that idea?"

"Because you seem different than you were in Ljubljana and New York. Like you're off your goddamn meds."

Adele shrugged. "I get this way when I am nervous. *Ungebunden.* Footloose is the English word, yes?"

"Other words come to mind." Harper shook her head. "Listen to me. I really can't do this shit anymore. Do you hear me? I can't. I must've been crazy to think I was going to just get you to the gates of that refugee camp and then just be able to go back to the hotel and wait and slurp martinis."

"But then you would have nothing to write about. Think of it this way. This has been a good way to begin a story, yes?"

Harper looked away to conceal her smile. Yeah, this was a good way to begin a story, she thought to herself. "I must be crazy," she said under her breath. She looked back at Adele. "Just promise me we're going back to Erbil a different way."

Adele pointed at a road sign that said Duhok 15 Km. "Thirty minutes. First, we check out the GPS location where Luke called from. With any luck, he is still there."

Harper took one more glance behind them. This story Adele kept promising wasn't close to being over. That voice in her head also told her that for better or for worse, that story was going to write itself without her help.

18

EUPHRATES RIVER, SYRIA
SAME DAY

Luke squatted in a clump of cattails as he watched the dinghy emerge from the gray blanket of fog that cloaked the river's surface. The small craft appeared vastly overloaded, every available space crammed with passengers to the point where the low gunwales were hardly visible. Refugees, he assumed. Several times during the night on their journey from Mosul, they had spotted them. Sometimes it would only be a head peering up from a drainage ditch; at other times, a mere flash of color in the brush at the edge of their headlights. Masoud remarked that they were concealing themselves the best they could to minimize the risk of being assaulted and robbed by roving militia.

Much of the drive had been over sparse and arid hardpan, at times their route only a mere suggestion of an actual roadway. The few villages they passed were dark and uninviting, and might have even been abandoned gauging from the lack of vehicles or any visible evidence of habitation. Driving at night had been grueling and tedious enough, the absence of any signage or landmarks rendering it even more so. They all shared driving duty except for Masoud who sat in the back seat constantly consulting his map and compass.

They had rendezvoused at dusk at a gas station on the outskirts of Mosul. It had taken most of the day for Masoud to arrange for help, giving

Luke time to make the rounds of hotels and NGO offices in Duhok in the off chance anyone might have seen Maggie. As expected, his search had proved fruitless, which only heightened his anxiety at the prospect that the French journalist's possible sighting of Maggie might have some validity.

The two Kurds Masoud had recruited had initially given Luke pause for neither of them seemed older than twenties at best. He was forced to remind himself that many of troops he had once ordered into combat had been that same age. Masoud assured him they were both battle hardened despite their age. Still their youth disconcerted him. The adage came to mind about there being bold soldiers and old soldiers, but no old and bold soldiers. There was a lesson there, he reminded himself.

It brought to mind something Harper had said when referring to journalists in conflict zones. His thoughts lingered on Sarajevo for a moment before he forced himself to file away the memory of that time and turn his attention back to Masoud as he briefed their new companions.

Luke knew something of the reputation of Kurdish fighters. Even the young woman conveyed an understated toughness and economy of move-ment Luke found reassuring. Jihan was her name, and she had once been a soldier in the Peshmerga. Wiry, with long coal black hair and not appearing a day older than eighteen, she had last seen action in the defeat of the ISIS effort to capture Erbil. She also happened to be Masoud's niece, and spoke fairly good English. She proudly admitted she had learned it from watching American cartoons as a child in Erbil.

The other Kurd was called Khalef. He was far more gregarious and talkative than Masoud although he spoke only a smattering of English. He too had once fought with the Peshmerga. They both seemed fit, and comfortable with what might be required of them. They also came well armed. He had watched them as they stowed two AK-47s, two an M-16s, a Remington 12 gauge shotgun, a brace of assorted Glocks, and a WELL G25 sniper rifle into the hidden compartment beneath the SUV's back seat. Their arsenal was reassuring, but even more reassuring was their demeanor. The prospect of crossing into Syria seemed not to concern them, even after they had told they might be undertaking a rescue mission with unknown risks. Of course, Luke had sweetened the pot by promising to pay them each four thousand dollars and a bonus if everything proved successful.

Their plan had been to drive through the night on back roads or even overland to avoid checkpoints. They hoped to reach the border while it was still dark, and then cross over and be at the river before dawn. Masoud assured Luke he knew the location of the village, and even knew of a nearby river crossing often used by refugees. Their route would initially take them west and past Sinjar and the nearby mountain where in 2014 ISIS had abducted and slain thousands of ethnic Yasidi civilians, most of them women and children.

From there, they would make their way south over open land that was relatively under populated, thus decreasing any risk of encountering PMG militia checkpoints. Masoud planned to cross the border just north of where the Euphrates crossed into Iraq. There they would secure a barge or a dinghy to cross the river, and then make their way up into the nearby hills to Tel Sayyid. Luke deferred to Masoud's judgment, seeing nothing from a tactical standpoint with which to disagree.

After leaving Mosul, Luke checked his iPhone and found a text message from Adele.

> *I saw your message but the reception was poor. I was unable to fully hear your plan. I am flying to Baghdad on the 24th, then to Erbil. Please tell me where you are. I have new and concerning information about M that I think best I not write here. Please respond. A*

He uttered a curse loud enough to draw the attention of the others. What in the hell did she think she was doing, he asked himself as he reread her text. This was just like her, to charge headlong into a situation she knew nothing about. Like more than few intelligence analysts he had encountered, they either didn't know or didn't care enough about the actual situation on the ground. Their over reliance on satellite and drone imagery in place of hard, firsthand intelligence often placed lives at risk. He and Adele's differences of opinion regarding this had often been an additional source of friction in their relationship.

And what did she mean about new and concerning information? About M? She meant Maggie. What had she found? If Maggie had finally surfaced, Adele would've told him. He started to text something back and then hesitated, unsure as to whether he should tell her anything before he had checked out the Syrian lead. One way or the other, he would likely know something by tomorrow morning. He would wait and text her then when he knew more.

It was still dark when they reached a point just a couple miles from the border. Giving into caution, Masoud thought it best to leave the SUV concealed on the Iraqi side and proceed on foot. They parked it in a thick copse of trees and further camouflaged it with branches and dead shrubbery. The hike to the border had been uneventful and hardly proved fatiguing as the terrain was relatively flat. After perhaps thirty minutes, they stumbled onto a dented and rusty metal sign affixed to a chipped concrete pylon. The words on the sign were in Arabic and hardly legible. The Syrian border, Masoud announced. From there, they pushed through the dense riparian foliage for another mile before breaking cover at the river's edge just as the sky began to lighten. Luke could make out the morning star and a half moon in an otherwise clear sky.

He now rose from his vantage point in the cattails and joined Masoud who had been watching the dinghy's approach from a small shed beside the crude landing dock. Jihan and Khalef had set up a perimeter in the nearby brush. Luke watched as the over laden dinghy nudged up to the dock. Before its pilot had even tied up, several of the refugees tumbled out and scampered up the muddy bank, and promptly disappeared into the chest-high thicket of reeds that lined the bank.

"It is very good," Masoud said, leaning into his cigarette. "*Mûj*, yes? The fog."

"You're sure this guy will take us across?"

Masoud made a balancing gesture with his hand. "You have money? Give him fifty dollars. He will take us."

Luke peeled off five tens from the stash in his waist bag and handed them to Masoud who strolled down the river bank to consult with the dinghy's owner. It was colder here in the river bottom, and Masoud had finally replaced his pea coat with a well worn and tattered down jacket. Jihan and Khalef emerged from the brush and joined Luke. There only accommodation to the cold were the mufflers worn around their necks. They carried small battle packs, a handgun strapped to their thigh, and each carried an AK47. Masoud had opted for an M-16, but also had brought along the sniper rifle in a padded camouflaged rifle case. As for himself, he took the other M16 and a Glock.

Luke began to grow impatient as Masoud seemed to take an inordinate amount of time negotiating for the crossing. Finally, he turned and motioned for them to join him on the small dock. The dinghy's captain turned out to be a stout young woman dressed in a man's fatigue tunic and wearing a ragged *hijab* that concealed her mouth but not her imperious green eyes. She scrutinized them for a several seconds before gesturing with a jerk of her head for them to climb into the dinghy. Luke found it necessary to push aside the detritus of food scraps, empty plastic water bottles, and bits of discarded clothing that littered the bottom.

The river was relatively placid; only the dimple of small eddies suggesting the presence of a current. Otherwise, the surface was as smooth and glassy as an eye. It felt surreal to glide through the mantle of fog, the only sounds that of birdsong and the gentle slapping of the oars. The river couldn't have been very wide for it took no more than eight or ten minutes to reach the far side. As they clambered out with their gear, Masoud paid the young woman who tucked the money into her jacket pocket and sat on the bank to await her next passenger.

"Did you tell her we may be back?"

Masoud nodded. "She is near," he said, gesturing with his thumb to a thick copse of reeds and what looked to be bamboo.

The riparian vegetation quickly gave way to a stony incline that rose steeply up towards a rumpled gray ridgeline silhouetted against the pinkish dawn. Even loaded down with a backpack filled with extra ammo, water, cold weather gear, and food, Luke had little difficulty keeping up with his younger companions. Retirement had not eclipsed the rigorous workout regimen that he had practiced every day since he entered West Point. In spite of his chain smoking, Masoud also seemed undeterred by the steep and narrow trail leading to the summit.

From a tactical standpoint, they should have approached the village in the dark, thus adding to any element of surprise. But their late arrival couldn't be helped. To make matters worse, Masoud had only a general idea of the village's location. They slogged their way to the top of the ridge and stopped atop a rocky outcrop that provided an expansive view of the countryside beyond. Luke could see what appeared to be several small villages and what might be some isolated farm houses scattered along the hillsides. Patches of fog obscured any appreciation of the low lying valleys. A dirt road snaked between them, disappearing and reappearing along the contours of the rolling terrain.

Masoud retrieved his binoculars from his pack and began scanning the road below, tracing its progress. After a moment, he paused to consider something, and then lowered the glasses and pointed along the ridgeline to the north.

"Tel Sayyid," he said, handing the binoculars to Luke.

Luke took them and peered in the direction Masoud had pointed. A mile or so down the ridgeline, he could see where the road led to a cluster of structures that were mostly the color of the surrounding stony landscape.

He could make out one or two white-washed buildings and what very well could be a water tower.

"You're sure?"

Masoud nodded. "Tel Sayyid," he said with effusive confidence and waved his arm for them all to follow him as he set off along the ridgeline at a maniac pace.

As they hiked along the narrow animal track that followed the ridge-line, Luke attempted to sort out in his mind the various scenarios, and what action he was prepared to take. He had no way of really knowing if Maggie was there of her own free will, or if she might be held captive. The extent of what Adele had shared with him was that Maggie's boyfriend, this Murat guy, had told Adele that he planned on visiting his family in Syrian Kurdistan, and that Maggie wished to see some of the camps for herself. He tried not to think of any possible reason why Maggie had neglected to call either of them. There should have been ample opportunity to find a cell connection or WiFi in the larger surrounding towns.

A thought suddenly occurred to him. Murat. What if Adele's mention in her text of the letter 'M' had referred to Murat and not Maggie? Did Adele know something more about the man that had led Maggie into this sorry situation? He brushed these more sinister possibilities aside as he attempted to match Masoud's purposeful stride.

19

The rising sun had just erased the shadows along the ridge as they drew within a couple of hundred yards of the village's outskirts. A goatherd, a young boy of perhaps ten or so, watched their advance with passive curiosity. Thin scribbles of smoke rose from several of the houses. Otherwise, there were no other obvious signs of activity.

Masoud paused for a moment to scan the village with his binoculars, and then turned to Luke and pointed at something on the far edge of the village. It looked like the water tower the French journalist had described. Luke took the binoculars and focused on the tower. He could just make out some kind of Arabic lettering in red scrawled across the tank. He nodded to Masoud.

Masoud led them along a path that skirted the backside of the village and along the slope of the ridge. Luke assumed Masoud's plan was to approach the house from the rear to avoid detection. Luke sensed the two young Kurds behind him hoist their weapons, their vigilance obviously heightened. Giving into caution, he racked a round into the M16 and grasped it with both hands.

The path slipped behind and below a barn-like structure that perched on the edge of the ridge just a few houses down from the water tower. Through the barn's slatted walls, they glimpsed a woman milking a goat. If she noticed them, she paid little heed. The path then angled upwards, its trajectory leading them to the water tower. It was just as the Frenchman had described it. A small house constructed of flat stone slabs sat just in front of the tower.

Masoud signaled Khalef and Jihan to move around to the rear of the house, and then nodded with his head for Luke to follow him. They approached along the side of the house, their backs flat against the wall, bending low to avoid a window. Masoud glanced around the corner and then gestured for Luke to take a look. It appeared to be the house the journalist had described. He saw the blue door, but no truck. And no visible sentry, either. Masoud took the lead, advancing cautiously to the front door. He paused at a partially opened window and gave a quick peek inside. He seemed to consider something and then leaned over to Luke and raised two fingers. He closed his eyes and tilted his head in a manner that Luke guessed was meant to indicate there were two people inside, both sleeping.

Masoud slipped the sniper rifle from his shoulder and set it against the wall, and then eased his way to the door and carefully pressed down the lever-like handle. He paused for a few seconds as the door started to make a loud squeaking sound, and then abruptly shoved it open and wheeled inside.

Luke rushed in behind him as Masoud shouted something in what Luke assumed was Kurdish. In the dim light, Luke could just make out several cots, two of which appeared occupied. A figure on one of them swung up to a sitting position and started to lunge for something on the chair beside him, but Masoud was too fast, knocking the man's handgun to the floor. Without hesitating, he struck the man in the face with the butt of the M16, sending him sprawling just as the man in the other cot stirred. The other man's look of bleary bewilderment quickly changed to one of alarm. Masoud yelled something and the man quickly raised his hands. Both of the men wore jeans and sweaters. The one Masoud had struck was tall and powerfully built, the other was slight and paunchy. Luke couldn't tell anything much from their features. They could be Kurds, Iraqi, Turks, or even Syrians for all he knew.

A few seconds later, Jihan appeared in a doorway that led into the rear of the house. She and Masoud conversed for a moment as Khalef went about inspecting the room, collecting several weapons and a cell phone. Jihan disappeared back into the rear of the house.

"No one is here," Masoud said, turning to Luke. "No woman."

Luke muttered a curse. "Ask them where she went."

Masoud leveled his rifle at the man he had knocked to the floor. "*Jin li ku ye?*" The man swiped at his bloody mouth and stared at Masoud as if not understanding. Masoud asked again, this time raising his rifle as if he were about to strike him again. The man raised his hands and rattled off something unintelligible. Masoud studied him for a moment before turning to Luke.

"This man is Turkish." He motioned to Khalef and said something to him in what Luke assumed was Kurdish. Khalef leaned down in front of the Turk, his face inches from the man's and asked him several questions in what Luke assumed was Turkish. The Turk smiled and shook his head. Khalef rose up, muttered something, and then brought his boot down violently onto the man's bare foot. The Turk doubled over, howling in pain. Khalef yanked him upright by his hair and then brought his boot down on the man's other foot. He screamed again and fell back against the cot. When Khalef again yanked him upright by the hair, the Turk yelled something that sounded like a curse and spat a mouthful of bloody phlegm at Khalef's face.

Luke looked over at the man in the other cot who was cowering and mumbling to himself, almost as if he were praying. "Ask him," Luke said to Khalef.

Khalef removed a large hunting knife from his belt and walked over to the man.

"No! No! Please!" the man shouted.

"Do you speak English?" Luke asked.

"Yes. Please," he said, raising his hands higher.

•

"Where is the woman? The American woman. Where is she?"

The man shot a glance at his companion who muttered something which earned him a kick from Masoud.

"They take her with them."

"Took her where?"

"I do not know."

Khalef brandished his knife in the man's face.

The man shrunk back. "I told you. I do not know where they went."

"The woman. Do you know her name?"

He shook his head.

Luke opened his iPhone and pulled up Maggie's picture and held it in the man's face.

"This is her, yes?"

The man nodded.

"Who took her?"

The other man yelled something and Masoud promptly struck him with his rifle butt hard enough to render him senseless.

"Emin. He take the woman," his frightened companion quickly offered.

"Emin? Where is Murat?" Luke asked.

The man again shook his head. "I do not know that name."

"You're sure?"

The man nodded.

Jihan suddenly reappeared from the rear of the house and said something to Masoud with what sounded like urgency. Masoud motioned with his head for Luke to follow him. The cramped back room appeared to be some sort of store room. Piles of grain had been stacked along one wall. It also seemed as if it had been used to shelter sheep or goats gauging from

•

the smell and the presence of the pellet -like droppings that had been hap-hazardly swept to the side. In the center of the room was an open trap door that appeared to have been covered by a canvas tarp.

Jihan stood above the opening and shined a flashlight down inside. Masoud and Luke leaned over to peer inside the shallow hole. A matting of straw had been pulled aside to reveal a couple of military type backpacks, one of which had been overturned to reveal several grenades and a small block of something the size of a cigarette pack and wrapped in plastic. Luke picked up the block and examined it.

"Do you know what this is?" Luke asked, holding it to the light. "Semtex. Plastic explosive."

Masoud picked up one of the knapsacks and held it to the light. There was something in Arabic stenciled across the back. "Syrian Army," Masoud said, pointing to the inscription. "This insignia," he said pointing at a patch sewn on the side. "Also Syrian Army."

"I thought these men were Turkish."

"There is something else," Jihan said. "I am not sure, but you should see."

She used the tip of her knife to stab a piece of crumpled paper that lay in the dirt. She held it at arm's length as she shined her flashlight on it. The sheaf of paper appeared to be a label of some sort. It was torn and the lettering only barely legible. He took Jihan's wrist and pulled it closer in order to read the lettering. The large bold letters GB stood out and below it was a long word and something in Arabic.

"Holy shit!" Luke exclaimed.

"What is it?" Masoud asked.

"Organophosphate. It's a nerve gas. Sarin."

"And there is this," Jihan said. "It was in the pack."

It took a moment for Luke to recognize what she was handing him was a pre-filled syringe like the type someone might use if they had an anaphylactic reaction of some sort. He held it to the light. "Atropine," he said. "It's an antidote."

What was Maggie mixed up in, he asked himself, fingering the syringe,

20

Luke sat on the bag of grain, holding in his hand the short length of duct tape he had found amongst the sacks of grain. He had almost casually dismissed the tape before noticing the knot of blonde hair stuck to one end. He felt a rush of emotion - searing anger, and then a suffocating dread. The thought of Maggie in the hands of these psychopaths only aggravated his sense of hopelessness.

Tossing the tape aside, he walked over to the shallow hole. He still felt stunned by what they discovered and its possible implications. He sat staring into the hole, only faintly aware of Masoud giving orders to Jihan who then brushed past Luke and disappeared out the crude doorway that led out the rear of the house. Masoud's hand on his shoulder jerked him back to awareness.

"Come, We must talk," the Kurd said, starting for the rear doorway without waiting.

Luke rose to his feet, his eyes still fixed on the Sarin label lying atop the backpack, and then followed Masoud outside. The morning sun had warmed the valley below, erasing the fog that had earlier cloaked the river. From here on the ridge, the path of the Euphrates resembled a dark scrawl as it wound through the verdant river bottom.

Masoud stood on the edge of the path, his gaze fixed on the river. He too had seemed visibly disturbed by the discovery, and like Luke, seemingly at a loss for words.

"What should we do?" Masoud said finally. When Luke shook his head, he went on. "Hussein used such a gas on my people. Many died. That son of a whore Assad has used it also."

"But these are Turks. Why would they have Sarin? They obviously plan on using it. But on who? Assad's troops?"

Masoud looked at him. "We will have Khalef ask them," he said sternly and walked back into the hut.

Luke followed him inside. The larger of the two Turks, the insolent one Masoud had earlier knocked senseless, had by now stirred and lay on his side, sneering up at them. The other one sat dejectedly on the cot, his head down and resting in his hands. Masoud said something to Khalef who began immediately interrogating them both in Turkish. The one on the cot whimpered and shook his head, too cowed and defeated to look at Khalef. The other one grinned up at Khalef through his broken teeth and then spat toward Masoud's feet. He yelled something at Khalef and attempted to kick him, but Khalef dodged him.

Masoud said something to Khalef and then before Luke could react, Masoud pulled his Glock from his waistband and shot the Turk in the face. The sound reverberated through the small room, all but drowning out the other Turk's wails.

Luke, too stunned to react, watched as Masoud stuck the handgun back into his waistband, and leaned down, his face inches from the face of the now screaming Turk on the cot.

"You will tell us now," he said softly, then repeated this louder to make himself heard over the Turk's bawling.

Luke squatted beside the man, and gently nudged Masoud aside. He gripped the Turk's face in his one hand, forcing him to meet his eyes.

"Shut up!"

The Turk flinched, his wails dying to a whimper.

"We need to know where they went. Do you understand? Where they went and what they were planning on doing. You tell me now or my friend will start with the knife. Okay?"

The man nodded, his eyes glazed with fear as he glanced up at Masoud. "I do not know where they went. I swear."

Luke let go of the man's face and nodded to Masoud who stepped up to Luke's side.

No!" the Turk screamed.

"Okay, then tell me where they went and what are they going to do."

The Turk took a deep breath and cleared his throat. "I am simply a driver. They tell me nothing. Wait! Wait!" he said when Masoud made to reach again for his knife. "I heard them speaking. They say they would drive to the refugee camps. I swear. That is all I know."

"Which camp?"

The man shrugged. "I did not hear which one."

"Do you know what they were going to do at the camp?"

The man's eyes darted back and forth frantically between Luke and Masoud's hand on the knife sheath.. He closed his eyes then in some resignation and shook his head. "They had some sort of gas. They will release it." He looked at Luke with a look of petty triumph. Luke resisted hitting him.

Luke stared at him for a long moment before forcing his eyes away. He thought then of Maggie and why this was happening. More than a few thoughts of bitter self-incrimination rose to mind before he grabbed the Turk's throat. He reached into his pocket with his other hand and removed the block of Semtex.

"Are they going to use this?" he asked, holding the Semtex in front of the man's face. He felt the Turk swallow several times before nodding.

"I will ask you only once more. Where? Which camp?"

The Turk struggled, trying to escape Luke's grip.

"I do not know. I told you. A camp they say. I know nothing more."

"When did they leave?"

"Early this morning. Before the daylight."

"How many men?" Masoud asked.

The Turk looked up at Masoud and then back at Luke. "Two men. And the woman," he muttered with obvious resignation. He hung his head and slumped like someone who realized he had cashed in his last chip,

Luke rose to his feet and turned to Masoud. "How many camps are there?"

"Many. Some are large. Bardarash. Some small. There could be many between here and the border of my province. It will take a great deal of time to check each one "

"Where would they cross into Iraq?"

He shrugged. "If they are in a truck? Abū Kamāl. It is not far. From there to get to the camps they will drive north much the same way we drove last night."

"A truck." Luke squatted back down in front of the man on the cot. "What kind of truck?"

The Turk looked up but said nothing. His last card, Luke thought, nodding up at Masoud, who leaned down and pinched the man's ear lobe.

"No! Please! I tell you. The lorry... the truck. A Mercedes military truck. You know. Off road with the big wheels."

"What color?"

"*Beyaz.* White."

"I'm giving you one more chance. Which camp? I'll bet you know. Don't lie."

The man sniffled and swiped at his nose. "I heard them say several names. But I hear them last night. Emin and Hassan. They say Bardarash."

Luke rose to his feet and turned to Masoud. "Do we take him with us?"

Masoud met Luke's eyes. "The Turks have killed many of my people. My wife's family. They murder them." He looked back at the Turk. "He cannot help us." He pulled out his Glock. The Turk began to whimper. Without the slightest hesitation, Masoud shot him in the head, knocking the man backwards onto the cot.

Luke turned away for a moment before staring down at the Turk. "We could've taken him."

"We have no time. We must go," was Masoud's only reply.

Almost as if on cue, Jihan burst through the front door and spat out a torrent of words at Masoud who quickly holstered his Glock and followed Jihan to the door.

"What's going on?" Luke asked.

"Militia. They heard the shots," Masoud said as he peeked out the partially open door.

"Whose militia?"

Masound shook his head. "Asssad. Hezbollah, maybe. We must leave now," he said calmly, taking up his M16 and swinging the sniper rifle over his shoulder.

Luke grabbed his own rifle and hurried to follow Masoud out the back door. As they started back down the path along the ridgeline, their presence concealed by the adjoining barn, they heard what sounded like at least two vehicles pull up in front of the house, followed by several yells. They quickened their pace, hoping to make the nearest slope on the ridge that might conceal them.

They had put about a hundred yards between them and the village when they heard shouting, and a second later, the distinctive plunking sound of a single round from an AK-47, followed by the rattle of the rifle on fully automatic. Another rifle joined in, and Luke could hear several rounds ricochet off the stony ground on either side of him. Another round passed just over his shoulder. His mind flashed to the Semtex in his pack and how fortunate it was that there wasn't a detonator attached to it. Hunched over, they threw themselves over the lip of a concealing slope, and then ran for the next position that might offer them protection.

Masoud hesitated for a second, and then instead motioned them to follow him down the steep hillside toward the river, obviously hoping to get them off the exposed ridge and into the concealment of the heavily vegetated river bottom. They probably had only a minute or so before their pursuers would breach the ridgeline above and no doubt spot them. They half-ran, half-stumbled down the rocky hillside. They were almost into the covering vegetation when they heard renewed bursts of rifle fire directed down at them.

Masoud swung the G25 sniper rifle off his shoulder and dropped into a kneeling position. Jihan and Khalef said something to him, but he waved them off as he racked a round into the rifle's chamber. Jihan grabbed Luke's arm and tried to pull him along with her and Khalef into the curtain of bamboo, but Luke pulled away.

"You go. Wait for us at the boat. You understand?"

He took his M16 and squatted in the scrubby grass a few yards from Masoud who had by this time propped his rifle in the crook of a nearby small tree. Luke could see several of the militia silhouetted on the ridge above them. Masoud took a few seconds to find them in the scope and then fired twice, and then twice more. To his satisfied astonishment, Luke saw two of their pursuers fall. The others fell back behind the ridge.

Masoud waited, his eye still glued to the rifle's scope. Several seconds later, two more figures appeared on the ridge. He promptly dropped one of them with one shot.

"We go now," he said and abruptly rose to his feet and ran for the bamboo. Luke followed.

They found Jihan and Khalef waiting at the crossing, the dinghy moored at their feet. The young woman who had brought them over was nowhere to be seen. They quickly boarded, and Jihan pushed them off as

Khalef began paddling. All the while, Masoud kept the sniper rifle at the ready as he scanned the shoreline. It seemed to take them longer to get across then previously, but the crossing was uneventful, the only casualty the block of Semtex Luke wisely, but much to Masoud's dismay, pitched over the side.

An hour later, after several failed attempts, they finally found their SUV. They spent only enough time to top off the gas tank, emptying the last of the jerry cans. With Jihan behind the wheel, they set out north. While Khalef and Masound downed a meal of bread and cheese, Luke checked his iPhone for any sign of a signal. One bar that was weak at best. He wasn't surprised to see Adele had left him several messages. It was the last one that caught his interest enough to read twice.

> *You have to know something. Murat is not who we thought. He's a Turkish intelligence agent who uses the name Emin Ozbek, Where are you? I am now in country and going to Duhok today. Please call. A*

He had the sense that Adele knew nothing about the Sarin, much less what this Ozbek might be planning. This revelation that Ozbek was a Turkish agent bewildered him. The unanswered questions swirled in his mind. Why would a Turkish agent be crossing into Iraq with a cache of Sarin gas? And where was he really headed? Then there was the still unanswered question of why Ozbek had taken Maggie with him. He tried to call Adele but not surprisingly, the call kept getting dropped. It would have to wait for some decent cell reception.

No one had spoken since leaving, each of them no doubt consumed by their successful escape from the militia, but also what might lie ahead. Now Luke had time to process what had occurred back in the village. There was no getting around the fact that Masoud had summarily executed the two Turks without a moment's hesitation.

Luke had served as an infantry soldier for almost thirty years, and a good third of that time spent in combat zones, and by his own hand he had only personally killed someone twice. Deaths as a result of his orders were a different and more troubling matter. Soldiers whose lives had been his responsibility died by his direction. Enemies, whose motives, morality or lack of it were out of his purview, died by his direction. And people who had no business dying had died in the name of war; in his name. It was that crime that still gnawed at him.

But as for deaths directly by his hand, there were only the two. The first one was a suicide bomber charging his convoy. A sergeant told him that didn't count because the crazy *haji* was going to die anyway. The second was a legitimate combat kill, a Taliban soldier who had been long on fervor and short on infantry tactics. At the time, neither of those two deaths had bothered him on any appreciable level. He was a soldier, he told himself. It was his job. It was only years later, that he began to dwell on those deaths. But even then, what he reflected on was more life's fragility and the finality of his actions, rather than the ethics of killing an enemy soldier.

Were Masoud's actions really any different? The easy answer was yes. But it was beyond him to accept, much less understand, the motives and ethos of people who hadn't known any real peace in decades, if not a lifetime. He had seen much the same in Sarajevo. The lines in these kinds of conflicts often became blurred, and the vagaries of circumstance made the possibility of his casting judgment more and more difficult.

He couldn't help but smile remembering the remark made by a fellow UN peace keeper from Texas when discussing their role in the Balkans.

"Don't you see that you just can't teach these people peace? It's like trying to teach a pig to sing. It's a waste of your time and just annoys the pig. And these people seem already pretty well annoyed."

Sometimes it seemed that simple. Maybe this was one of those times. He just wondered how many more fatal judgments and retributions would be rendered in the next few days.

21

DUHOK

The crossing into Duhok had proved uneventful. However, the Peshmerga border guard gave them the once over when he noted the SUV's shattered windows, but said nothing. They both felt secure being back in Kurdistan and not having to worry about bandits, if that's what their pursuers had been. They may have just as likely been Shia outliers looking to harass Westerners in the hope of nothing more than a shakedown.

As soon as they entered the city, Adele entered the GPS location from where Luke had ostensibly called from. The GPS took them to an older part of the city hemmed in on one side by a mountainside, and on the other, by a warren of narrow streets and bazaars. Even with the GPS, it took them a half hour to pinpoint the location. From what Adele could tell, the signal had originated from a grouping of two and three story buildings that housed shops and what appeared to be upstairs residences gauging from the clotheslines crisscrossing the street.

As Adele started to turn off her phone, she saw someone had tried to call. It was Luke's number, but there was neither a text nor a voice mail. She redialed but all she got was a strange tone that perhaps indicated there wasn't any reception. She muttered a curse. The missed connections were becoming annoying. She looked at the time of the call. Ten o'clock that morning. He had probably called in the midst of their escape. She slipped the phone into her shirt pocket so she would hear it in case he called again.

They parked the Land Cruiser in front of a police station in the hope it would be safeguarded, and began walking in the vicinity of the signal. The best candidate for their search turned out to be a small, seedy looking hostel with the curious name of "Dalai Lama Respite".

The lobby, such that it was, stood empty other than a pair of large backpacks propped against a wall. The reception desk, a simple wooden plank atop two shipping crates, was bare except for an ancient-looking ledger and a small brass temple bell. Faded photographs of Lhasa and the Himalaya covered the adobe brick wall behind the desk. Adele rang the bell several times. A minute later, a short elderly woman, most likely Tibetan gauging from her features, appeared seemingly out of nowhere.

"Do you speak English?" Adele asked.

The woman smiled and nodded. Her face looked as weathered and sun beaten as the adobe brick wall behind her. Her rheumy gray eyes looked even older than her face.

"We are looking for someone, a man, an American, who might have stayed here."

When the old crone failed to react, Adele pulled out her iPhone and found a photo of Luke.

"This man. Was he here?" she asked, holding the phone up close to the woman's face.

She squinted and studied the image for what seemed an eternity before nodding. "Yes, he stay here," she said in a reedy voice.

"He's here now?"

She shook her head. "No. He leave." She pulled the ledger toward her and painstakingly opened it, and just as methodically began to page through it. Her sluggish progress almost prompted Adele to take the ledger away from her and search on her own.

"Yes," the woman said finally, peering closely at a page. She looked up at Adele but said nothing more.

"Yes, what? *Gott!* When did he leave?"

"Yesterday." The old woman leaned closer to the ledger, her bony index finger pointing at something. "He leave yesterday afternoon."

"Did he say where he was going?"

She shook her head and smiled.

"*Fick!* We missed him by a day." She looked at Harper. "Well, I guess he has either left Duhok or felt he needed a hotel upgrade."

"So now what?"

"We could go to Bardarash."

"And take the chance of meeting up with those guys whose pick up you trashed? I don't think so."

"Let us go have a beer and think about it." Adele turned to the old woman. "Is there someplace nearby where we can eat?"

She stared at Adele for a moment as if not comprehending before retrieving a small card from beneath the desk and handing it to her. "One street," she said, pointing with her bony finger in a direction that was difficult to ascertain.

The crumpled business card stated something in Kurdish, and beneath it in parentheses, the title "The Blood Of My Favorite Ox", and below that a telephone number. Adele flipped it over to find a map that promised to be less than helpful. They wandered down a narrow street in what seemed the direction the woman at the hotel had indicated. Sure enough, a block later they spotted a wooden sign with the identical title in Kurdish as was on the card.

The small dining room appeared packed with a lunch time crowd, mostly Kurds from the looks of it. They settled into the only empty table and signaled the waitress, a young girl who seemed no older than perhaps twelve. They ordered two beers and what seemed to be the soup de jour, some sort of goat stew from what they could tell from the menu description.

Adele checked her phone again. There were still no messages. She was half-tempted to try to reach her friend at Langley and ask for help.

As they ate in silence, Adele found herself wondering if Harper's commitment was waning, especially after this morning's incident. Not that she could blame her. It didn't bode well for driving around the countryside when they encountered a possible hijacking in an area that was considered relatively safe.

When the waitress brought their bill, Adele pulled out her phone. "Excuse me," Adele said to the waitress. She found Luke's photo and held it up to the girl. "Have you seen this man?'

The waitress leaned closer to study the image. "Yes. This man here. Two day ago."

"Was he by himself? Alone?"

"Yes, by self. But I see him talk to that man," she said, pointing to a man sitting alone in the corner. He wore a bulky cable knit sweater and a Greek fisherman's cap that failed to conceal his long, tousled red hair.

Adele stood and approached the man's table. She could see he was immersed in something on a small laptop. After a moment, he looked up and stared at Adele.

"The waitress said you spoke to this man," she said, showing him Luke's photo.

Before looking at it, he gave Harper an appraising glance as she joined Adele. He studied the photo for a second and nodded. "Sure. The Yank who was looking for a woman.

Adele scrolled down on the phone. "This woman?" she asked, holding out the phone.

"Yeah, at least she's the one my mate thinks he saw."

"Do you have any idea where he might have gone?"

"Maybe Syria. We were laying low in this shit shingle of a place on other side of the Euphrates. Waiting to cross over, you see. "

Adele had a bit of difficulty understanding what he said because of his Cockney accent.

"Your friend saw her there in this village. He was sure?"

"I've got no reason not to believe him. I think this Yank was planning on going there to look for her."

"This place. You said it's in Syria?" Harper interjected.

"Yeah, Just across the border. A village called Tel Sayyid. That night after we talked with your friend, we tried to figure out where this place was. You see, we only saw it in the dark, coming and going. It wasn't much of a town. A dozen houses at the most and probably too small to be on any maps.

"So where was it?"

"The best we could tell, it's in these hills just across the Euphrates. If you have map, look for a place called Abū Kamāl. We thought this village was a bit north of there."

"He was going there? By himself?"

"Dunno."

"Your friend saw this young woman? What did he say she was she doing there?"

"He said he saw her with some men in front of this house. The house had a water tower behind it is all I recall my mate saying."

"With some men," Adele repeated. What in the hell are you doing Maggie, she thought to herself. And why hasn't Luke told me about this? Maybe that was what he was trying to call her about this morning. Maybe he had found her.

Adele retrieved a road map from her coat pocket and unfolded it in front of the man. "Show me where you think this village is located."

He leaned over the map and traced over it with his finger. "Here is Abū Kamāl. This village is here roundabouts from what we could tell," he said, pointing at a blank space on the map. "It's a good ways from here. Easily six or more hours drive south."

Adele looked at the map. There didn't appear to be much in the way of roads leading to that part of the border. "Thank you," she said, folding the map.

"I know you," the man said, nodding at Harper. "I've seen your picture." He closed his eyes as if to concentrate. "Yeah, you're Harper Harris, right? The journalist?"

Harper smiled but didn't reply.

"In the flesh. Well, half-inch me. I'm an admirer. I'm a free lance photographer of sorts. The name's Ian," he said, offering Harper his hand. "Heading to Syria, are you? I know the way," he said with a laugh. "You birds need a guide?"

"I don't think so," Adele said. "But thanks for the offer and the information."

She took Harper by the arm and led her out the door.

"You're not seriously thinking of trying to go there?" Harper asked.

"It's my only lead."

"Look at the map again, Adele. It's a long way over a lot of big empty. The chances of you finding Luke are slim. It would be pure luck. It's insane."

Adele checked her phone again. There was still nothing from Luke. She punched in his number and listened. And still no reception. Was he on his way back? Harper was right. Driving to the border wouldn't be easy. And it would be dark for much of the way, increasing the chance they would miss each other.

"Maybe he will call," she said. "Maybe he found her."

"I say sit tight and wait for him to call again," Harper said.

Adele took out the road map and spread it out on the hood of a nearby parked car. Harper was right about there not being many roads. Luke could be anywhere or nowhere. She just needed him to call. But what if he didn't?

"No," she said, folding the map. "I will drive until it is dark and then wait. By then, perhaps he will have called. It's not necessary for you to come."

"Meeting him half way isn't going to accomplish anything. You should wait here. Who knows if there's even decent cell phone coverage out there. "

She again realized that Harper was right. If only she get word to Luke about Ozbek. So she would wait.

Harper didn't say anything more until they reached the SUV. "We should find a hotel," she said, climbing in the passenger side.

"Why don't you look for one. I will be right back."

"Where are you going?"

"Into the police station. Perhaps they have a better map. I will be right back."

Adele entered the station and opened up her phone and began searching for the number. She needed help. Maybe her friend at Langley would be willing to shed some light on what was happening. She needed to know how Ozbek fit into this. She looked at her watch. It was early evening in Virginia. She punched in the number and waited. After four rings, he answered.

"I don't want to talk to you," he said without waiting for her greeting. "I mean it. You've compromised me enough already."

"I just need to know what is happening. Please."

There was hesitation and then she heard him clear his throat. "I'm sorry. I can't help you. Don't call me again," he said and hung up.

"*Scheisse*,"she muttered. She stood there a moment and considered her options before realizing she had none. Luke was their only chance. When she got back out to the SUV, she took one more glance at the street in both directions and got in.

"Where did you get this?" Harper said angrily. She lifted the handgun out of the handbag and brandished it in front of Adele's face.

"I brought it with me. Don't worry. I checked beforehand," she said, wrenching it from Harper's grasp. "They told me it was unlikely they would check my bag at the customs in Baghdad."

"They? Who is they?"

"Someone who knows. It is no matter. What is done is done." She held the gun in her lap and examined it as if seeing it for the first time. "Heckler und Koch VP9. Do you know it is considered the BMW of handguns?" she said, shoving it back into her handbag.

Harper looked at her in disbelief and shook her head. "Now I know you're insane. Do you even know how to use it?"

"Come, Harper. I was in the army. I served a tour in Afghanistan."

"What I meant was have you ever had to use it?"

Adele thought for a moment. If she was truthful in her reply, how would Harper react? "It is for an emergency," she said, finally.

"This is not my thing. Not anymore," Harper said, "I can't," she said, flinging open her door and climbing out. She stormed to the rear of the SUV and tried to open the locked door. "Open the back goddammit," she yelled.

Adele hit the unlock button and turned and watched as Harper removed her duffle bag and day pack.

"Where are you going?"

"Screw you, Adele. I'm not going to be a part of this. You go ahead and go by yourself. Then I'll know for sure you're off your fucking meds. *Wiedersehen*," she said and started off down the street.

Adele watched as Harper disappeared in the crowd of pedestrians before turning on the ignition. She sat there for a long moment staring at nothing more than the back of the truck parked in front of her.

"*Ja. Ich bin verr* Harper was right about that, too. She lowered her head onto the steering wheel and started to cry. It had been a long time since she had felt this helpless. She had always prided herself on her ability to manage anything that came her way; everything except the collapse of her marriage, that is. Ever since the breakup with Luke, she had been an emotional wreck, adrift and unfocused. It was partly the reason she hadn't intervened when Maggie became involved with Ozbek.

If something happened to Maggie, she would never forgive herself. She swiped at her eyes. It will be all right, she told herself. Luke has found her. She couldn't help but wonder again about Ozbek and the CIA's interest in a Turkish spy. There was obviously more to this than met the eye. Just so it didn't interfere with their effort to find Maggie.

"Come on, Luke. Call me," she said, checking her phone again.

She sat there for perhaps another couple of minutes rolling over in her mind her options, the risks. As much as she didn't want to admit it, she needed Harper. She adjusted the rear view mirror, scanned the street behind her once more, and then started off after Harper,

PART FOUR

"Love is like a brick. You can build a home with it,
Or you can use it to sink a body "
-Lady Gaga

22

NINAWÂ PROVINCE
WESTERN IRAQ

Masoud handed the binoculars to Luke and pointed. "You see. There by the wadi."

Luke adjusted the focus and scanned the desolate, semi-arid landscape until he found the patch of green. He could make out what appeared to be a patchwork of tents of varying sizes and colors partially concealed in the clump of date palms and stunted shrubs. There were perhaps twenty tents, along with some vehicles of different types, several of them trucks.

"Syrian refugees, I think," Masoud said. "They flee Assad. Most come to seek shelter in the camps, but many simply hide the best they can."

This was the third such settlement they had encountered. While the camps had varied in size and in the nationality of its denizens, they all seemed to lack much in the way of simple creature comforts. Invariably, the occupants consisted of mostly women, children and old men. They had checked out each of the camps for any sign of Ozbek or the truck, but had come across no sign of either.

On the primitive roadway leading north, they had encountered several small groups of refugees transiting on foot, along with the occasional truck carrying mostly produce or goats. Their investigations resulted in reports of various sightings of trucks, none of which matched the description the

Turk in the village had provided. A goatherd beside the road had provided them with a detailed description of what sounded like the right truck, but then added that it had been driving south, in the direction from where they had just come. Once, they came upon a truck parked beside the road that roughly matched the description, but it proved to be a government survey team scouting possible new routes.

"We will go see," Masoud said, taking the binoculars from Luke.

They approached the camp slowly as to not cause alarm. As they drew near, Luke could make out the vehicles well enough to determine Ozbek's truck wasn't amongst them. They pulled up perhaps fifty meters from the camp's edge, and he and Masoud climbed out and began walking toward the camp. Two men armed with automatic rifles emerged from behind one of the trucks and yelled something. Masoud answered back, and the two men seemed to relax,

"They are Kurds, Come," he said, walking toward them.

Luke followed, all the while the two men studied him warily. As Masoud spoke with them, Luke walked closer to the encampment. The tents, many of them consisting of no more than large canvas tarps, looked as if they would provide little protection from the cold or rain. A string of goats were tethered to one of the trucks. As he drew within ten or so meters, several more men appeared, all of them well armed and younger than any of the males they encountered in the previous camps. Giving into prudence, Luke stopped, content to observe from a distance.

A few curious children emerged from amongst the tents, only to be pulled back by the women. They seemed ill-dressed for the weather which had grown noticeably colder over the course of the day. The clear morning sky that had earlier allowed them a view of the snow-capped mountains above Duhok had given way to a thick gray cloud and a biting wind that carried with it the smell of goat scat, wood smoke, and the sour tang of misery. Luke turned and joined Masoud who was still conversing with the two men.

"These men are Syrian Democratic Force. Anti-Assad. They are trying to bring their families to safety in Erbil. Then they return to fight. They do not wish to go to the camps because the Iraqis control most of them. These men will not give up their weapons."

One of them, a slightly built man of perhaps thirty, nodded in agreement. A soiled bandana only partially obscured the fact the man was missing his left eye. A thick, ragged scar ran the length of his face, and another scar on his neck snaked into the upturned collar of his fatigue jacket. He wore a pair of binoculars around his neck.

"They saw a truck, A white truck. It passed by here perhaps an hour and a half ago."

"Can we be sure it was the one we're looking for?"

Masoud shrugged. "We cannot. But this one with the binoculars said he got a good look. He says it was an unusual truck. New, he said."

The man with the scar said something to Masoud, who bowed his head slightly.

"They have invited us for tea," Masoud said,

"And I'll bet you're going to tell me next that it would not be polite to say we have no time."

Masoud turned back to the man and began a lengthy monologue that his fellow Kurd responded to with a smile and a nod of his head. Masoud gave the man a salute and turned for the SUV.

"So what did you tell them?" Luke said, catching up with him.

"I thanked him and told him we had to kill some Turks before darkness, and we had no time for tea." When Luke grunted in reply, he went on. "These are the people this Turk wishes to gas," he said with obvious bitterness.

"I understand that the Turks and your people are enemies. But it still doesn't seem to make sense. I mean, why would this Ozbek…why would Turkey want to attack the camps?"

"It is because of their hatred for my people. And they wish to destroy the PKK. The stronger Kurdistan becomes, the more we are a threat."

"I thought after the invasion there was some kind of alliance between Turkey and the anti-Assad Kurds."

"We have a saying. We Kurds have no friends but the mountains."

"Still, it seems a big risk. If Ozbek was one of Assad's people it would make more sense. For one thing, Assad's used poison gas before, and I'm sure he would like to eliminate any of the Syrian rebels, Kurds or not. There're a couple of more things that don't make sense. The backpacks and the gas, for instance. They had Syrian Army markings. And why did he come so far south before crossing into Iraq when most of the camps are up north?"

Masoud didn't reply. When they reached the SUV, he paused and pulled out a map which he spread atop the hood. He studied it for a moment before looking back at the camp. "I do not believe these camps are the places he is going to attack. He must want the large camps."

"Like Bardarash."

"Yes, there will be more deaths."

Luke thought back to their visit to Bardarash. It seemed longer ago than just three days. The number of refugees, the density of the camp, and their overall vulnerability made perfect sense. If Ozbek wished to inflict the greatest number of death it would mean poisoning a camp like Bardarash.

"Then let's head to Bardarash," Luke said, starting to turn away.

"They will not go on the roads if possible," Masoud said, still bent over the map. "And they will not go near Mosul. There will be too many Iraqi checkpoints. The same if they go to Sinjār. This way," he said, tracing his finger across the map. "They will go overland. Less risk. Risk is the word, yes? Their truck can do this. It will take longer but less chance of checkpoints."

"Then I guess we should go that way, too." Luke looked at this watch. "It's three now. We have … What? Maybe three hours at the most before dark? Do you think we can catch them before then?"

"I will drive first." Masoud replied, pushing Khalef aside and climbing behind the wheel.

Luke piled in the back and took up the map and Masoud's compass. Gauging from the map, it didn't seem likely that they or Ozbek would make it to Bardarash until long after dark. That was probably what Ozbek was counting on.

It occurred to him that they still had time to warn someone. He regretted not asking McDermott for her cell number. The chances of finding a UNHCR phone number somewhere with a live person on the other end seemed unlikely. Could he warn the authorities in Mosul? The Iraqi National Police, perhaps? Something told him they either wouldn't believe him or disregard him out of semi-benign ambivalence. He also had no idea if any US troops remained in Mosul, much less how he could possibly reach them. That left Adele. As much as he didn't want to admit it, she might be their only chance. If she was truly in Duhok, maybe she could get to the camp and warn them in time. He took out his phone. No bars. They would have to get closer.

They set out once again, leaving the road behind them and speeding across the rough open terrain in a desperate attempt to make up for lost time. All the while, Luke couldn't erase Maggie's plight from his mind. He had to find her before Ozbek had time to initiate his plan. And why was he keeping her? That is if she was still really with him. All he could come up with was that Ozbek was using her to gain access to the camps. And would Ozbek still need her if they arrived at the camp during the night?

Adele was their only hope. On the one hand, he had little doubt she was capable of the task required of her. On the other hand, she was headstrong and often acted impulsively. And would he be able to contact her in time?

He compulsively checked his phone again. If something happened to Maggie, neither of them would forgive the other, much less themselves. He put away his phone and began studying the map.

23

Harper stepped out of the liquor store clutching a bottle of some rotgut Bulgarian gin only to find Adele parked in front. Adele lowered the window and smiled. Harper stood there a moment before walking up to the Land Cruiser.

"How did you know where I was?"

"I took a guess. You cannot miss the sign," Adele replied, pointing at the large sign above the sidewalk that announced simply 'Liquor' in several languages. "Actually, I saw you go inside. Get in. Please."

Harper shifted the duffle bag on her shoulder, opened the door, but made no effort to get in. "Not until you tell me what's really going on."

"Sehr gut. Keine mehr Spielen und Spass,"

"Dammit, Adele. English, please."

"I said no more fun and games then. Okay? Please get in. It is cold."

Harper tossed her day pack and duffle in the back seat and started to climb in. "First, tell me where we're going."

"We should find a hotel. We should have a bath, room service, and your alcohol. What do you have? Gin? That will do."

"I guess this means you've decided to wait for Luke to call."

Adele sighed. "Yes. That is all I can do unfortunately." She took a moment to scan the street behind her in both the mirrors.

"You're still looking to see if we're being followed, aren't you?"

"I will tell you when we get to the hotel. Why don't you find us one?" she said, glancing at her watch. "It is almost four," she said, pulling out into the traffic. "We need a place with good cell phone reception."

While Adele drove, Harper called several hotels. She finally settled on the Rixos, judging it on nothing more than the pictures of the food on their website. In a matter of forty five minutes they were in their room on the fourteenth floor. The spacious, well appointed room afforded a view of an adjoining steep, rocky hillside but little else. In the time it took for them to find the hotel, it had started to rain, further dimming what remained of the weak, late afternoon sunlight.

While Adele took a shower, Harper checked her emails. Funaya had checked in with the usual newsy school stuff. She ended her message with the question, "Are you helping find the daughter?" No queries about where she was or whether she was safe. Harper's agent had sent a message wondering why Harper hadn't returned his phone calls. Manny had left a voice mail that said simply "The Turk is radioactive. Stay away."

What did that mean? She tried calling him back, but he didn't answer. She poured herself a tumbler of gin, added a splash of soda and sat on the bed to wait for Adele to get out of the bathroom. This whole experience was beginning to be more than she bargained for. There were too many unknowns for one thing. And after the incident on the road from Erbil, she had little inclination to travel with Adele any further unless it was back to Erbil, and only then on the main road. The fact that Luke hadn't contacted Adele was worrisome to say the least. She agreed with Adele that Luke not calling seemed out of character with the man she knew, or thought she knew.

She heard the shower turn off, and when after almost ten minutes had gone by and Adele hadn't emerged, she tapped on the door. When she received no response, she knocked again.

"Adele. Would you like me to make you a drink?"

There was still no answer. Harper opened the door a crack and peered in. Adele was sitting on the edge of the tub, nude except for a towel draped across her shoulders. She held her head in her hands and was obviously sobbing. Harper pushed open the door, hesitated a moment, and then sat on the toilet beside her.

Adele swiped at her puffy eyes and looked at her. Her wet hair clung to her head like a helmet. "Maggie is dead," she said, hoarsely. "Isn't she?"

"You don't know that."

"*Ach*! *Drei Wochen. Verstehst du nicht?* Three weeks and no word. Missing in a place like this can mean only one of two things. She is either dead or she is a prisoner somewhere. *Gott.*"

Harper didn't know what to say. The same thought had already crossed her mind.

Adele took the glass from Harper's hand and took a long swallow. "I am pathetic," she said, finishing it off.

"You're human."

"*Ach. Ein Mensch.* Yes, I am human. That is so reassuring."

"Get dressed, and I'll make you a drink."

A minute or so later, Adele came out wearing a bathrobe. She looked older without her makeup; older or just beaten down. Harper couldn't tell which. She took the drink Harper offered her and dropped onto the bed.

"I never told you but I found Maggie in an orphanage. The place was…a shit hole is the expression Luke often used. Yes? There was no other way to describe it." She downed half of the gin in one swallow. "Maggie was emaciated, filthy. And afraid. I was also afraid. Afraid because I was uncertain as to why I was taking her. I realized that I needed her even more than she needed me. Do you understand what I am saying?"

"Yeah, I do. My therapist said becoming a mother is the ultimate gesture of optimism. I always thought wanting a child was the ultimate gesture of selfishness. Or desperation." Harper poured herself some more gin, forgoing the soda and ice. "The night I met Funaya I was riding in an ambulance in Freetown. Sierra Leone. We were picking up bodies. Ebola victims. Her mother was dying in the back of this ambulance, and the driver stuck Funaya in the front seat next to me. At that point, I wanted nothing more than a long shower and to leave godforsaken Africa. I didn't realize it until later that I needed her. I needed to feel something again. I had just had this cancer scare. At that point, I don't know what O was ,more afraid of. Facing my mortality or realizing I was alone and needing someone."

Adele offered her a weak smile. "Neither of us it seems chose motherhood for the purest of motives. No? Did you never wish to have children of your own?"

Harper hesitated before replying. It wasn't the time for gin fueled confessions, she thought and took a swallow of the warm gin. "Not after Sarajevo. They said I wouldn't be able to conceive again." She glanced at Adele to see if she had caught the word 'again'.

Adele nodded in sympathy. "Luke and I tried without success. And then came Maggie." She finished off her drink and handed the empty glass to Harper for a refill. "I fear I have failed her."

Instead of taking the empty glass, Harper took Adele's hand, unsure what to say.

"She is a good daughter," Adele said. "She cares for me. Despite how much I tried to change her, to mold her to suit my liking."

"I need food," Harper said in an attempt to lighten the mood. She had no need to dwell further on her own shortcomings and secrets. "I looked at the menu. The lamb brochettes sound good."

Adele nodded. "I will call. You take your shower."

"First you tell me who it is you think is following us."

"No one is following us. I am quite certain."

"But?"

Adele held out the empty glass. Harper poured her a small amount and waited.

"I believe I made a serious error in judgment. I called someone I knew at Langley to see if they could provide more information on Ozbek. All I know is that for some reason my inquiry alerted someone. A red flag went up is how it was put." She proceeded to tell Harper about the encounter at the airport with Graham.

"Wait. Why would the CIA wet their pants over someone asking about Ozbek?"

Adele shrugged. "Who knows? All that concerns me now is that Maggie may be with him. I just wish I knew why." She shook her head in despair.

The fact that the CIA was interested in Ozbek did little to assuage Harper's own misgivings. There obviously was more to this story than she realized. It forced her to ask herself again if the possibility of a story was the only reason she was still here. It occurred to her then that she had come along for all the wrong reasons. She hated to admit it, but at this point her curiosity overrode any sense of obligation or altruism. And where did closure with Luke fit in? She wasn't sure anymore. All she knew was this was quickly turning into a fool's journey. She left Adele to her own self-recriminations and went to take a shower.

The gin bottle was half-empty before room service was delivered. While they wolfed down their lamb, Adele talked Harper into regaling her with stories of her travels and assignments, a request that thanks to the lubricating effects of the gin, Harper was more than happy to oblige. Harper was just about to recount how she and the ATF agent Harlan Quist ended up in Liberia when Adele's phone chirped.

Adele lunged for it, knocking over her glass of gin. She glanced at the phone and looked at Harper.

"It's Luke."

24

Maggie hunched down as far as her bindings allowed in an attempt to flex her legs in the narrow cramped space of the truck bed. The crates piled on three sides of her prevented her from doing much more than flipping from one side to another. The cold coupled with two hours in this awkward position only exacerbated her already stiff joints. Hassan had casually tossed a blanket over her at their last rest stop, but it had long since slipped down to her feet.

She lost track of time, intermittently dozing in spite of the pot-holed and deeply rutted road. At times, she sensed they were driving cross country, through ravines, and up and down uneven hillsides. Gauging from her own inner clock and the patch of fading skylight visible above her, she thought it was near dusk. That meant it had been ten hours since they left the village above the river. However, it seemed only half of that time had been spent driving. Murat, or Emin, or whatever his name was, had stopped a half-dozen times. She surmised that he or Hassan possessed a bladder the size of a walnut. Unfortunately, they had not allowed her the same luxury of a potty break. The last time they let her out of the back of the truck had been at what passed for lunch time; cold tea, dried pita, and some goat cheese that tasted as if it had been aged only a week.

They had left the village just before dawn. Hassan had tied her hands with padded wrist restraints which he then secured to a steel frame behind the truck's cab. She had watched as they loaded several dozen sacks of rice followed by crates of potatoes and onions. Hemmed in, she was only able to see a slender rectangle of sky above her.

Just like her previous attempts to question Murat as to why she was being held captive, her pleas that morning had fallen on deaf ears. They were going to the camps is all he would reveal. None of this made sense. She had lain there awake most nights out of simple fear and anxiety, but also out of confusion as she ruminated as to what might be Murat's end game. It was all too bizarre; the change in his behavior, his choice in companions, their secretive border crossing and the change of houses, and her obvious captivity. Then there had been the visit yesterday by a slender older man who spoke to Murat in what sounded like Arabic. Unguarded, she had watched through a crack in the shuttered window as the man handed Murat a pair of olive drab backpacks, the kind carried by soldiers.

Her imagination ran wild with notions of some nefarious smuggling plot or something even more criminal, the exact nature of which still eluded her. As she passed from fitful sleep to dark panic and back again, she thought of her life back in Munich and of her parents who she feared she might never see again. And to what end? To be trussed like some animal in the back of a truck headed for God knows where and for God knows why, all due to a romantic delusion and impulsive sense of adventure? Her despair alternated with anger as she tried to figure a way out of this.

Unable to endure her full bladder any longer, she resorted to banging the back of her head against the rear of the cab. The manner in which they had tied her prevented her from raising her head high enough to peer into the truck cab's rear window. She sensed rather than saw Murat look at her. A few minutes slipped by, and the truck slowed and then came to a stop.

She heard both doors open, and a moment later, the sound of the crates at her feet being shifted aside. Murat scrambled over the bags of rice, leaned over her and released her wrist restraints.

"You must relieve yourself? Then quickly," he said with obvious irritation.

Her legs felt so stiff she could hardly move, so he helped her, dragging her across the sacks and down onto the ground. She stood there a moment attempting to get some feeling back into her legs. The sun was just beginning to set over a low range of dun-colored hills. They were driving north, that much she could ascertain. The air was cold and crisp, the faint wind moist with the smell of rain.

She watched as Hassan stepped to the side of the road and began to urinate. Murat grabbed her arm and in spite of her numb legs, hustled her to the opposite side of the road. He led her for twenty or so yards across the rocky, arid ground to a place where some low shrubs offered some semblance of privacy.

Murat gestured with his head for her to do what she needed to do. When she hesitated, he stepped closer.

"I have seen you piss before. You have nothing to hide. So, go," he said, shoving her towards a clump of brush festooned with bits of torn newspaper and plastic bags. From the acrid smell, she guessed this place served as a roadside toilet. She stumbled a few steps forward and then loosened her pants and did her best to squat. The ground before her was littered with food wrappers, rusty cans, and broken glass. Next to her foot, half-hidden in the foul dirt, she spied the jagged and broken neck of a Coke bottle along with a few other shards of glass. She glanced over her shoulder at Murat who had turned away to relieve himself.

As she peed, she pried one of the glass shards loose and slipped it carefully into one of the leg pockets of her cargo pants. Glancing back, she saw Murat was still turned away. She picked up the three inch long neck of the broken Coke bottle and hid it in the palm of her right hand.

"Hurry, woman!" Murat yelled.

She staggered to her feet, pulled up her pants with her free hand and then turned toward Murat who stood watching her.

"What are you doing, Murat?"

"I told you. You shall call me Emin."

"Tell me something, Emin," she said, repeating his name with obvious disdain. "Was everything we shared in Munich just a lie to get me here? All of those I love you's. All of it was just bullshit. You're a fucking asshole. And I'm a bigger one for ever believing you had any feelings for me."

He laughed. "You are a foolish woman, Maggie. Come now, let us go."

He reached for her arm, and as he did, she swung at him with the broken bottle neck. Caught off guard, he jerked back, raising his arm to block her. He winced as the jagged glass sliced into his forearm.

"*Orospu!* You stupid bitch!" he yelled, clutching at his arm.

She tried to swipe at him again, but he quickly grabbed her wrist and twisted it, forcing her to drop the shard. She dropped to her knees and struggled to find it in the loose dirt. He kicked her in the side, knocking her back on her heels. As she struggled to regain her footing, he grabbed her by the collar of her jacket, and started to drag her back to the truck. Stumbling to her feet, she cursed him in between gasps of air. He pushed her down onto the dusty, rutted roadway and yelled at Hassan who quickly appeared from around the side of the truck. As Hassan replaced her wrist restraints, Murat studied the blood streaming down his arm before stripping off his shirt. As he wrapped one of the sleeves around the wound, he looked at her.

"I am Emin. Murat is no more," he said coldly. He started to turn away and then stopped. "Yes, I had feelings for you. If not, I would've given you to the others after we crossed the border. Be grateful for that. For it is all you have left." He said something to Hassan who dragged her back up into the truck and tied her wrists tightly to the crossbar behind the cab.

"The blanket," she said, but he either didn't understand or ignored her as he stacked the crates around her. A minute or so later, they started back down the road.

It must've been no more than an hour later, the dusk now having given way to nightfall, the dark sky devoid of anything so much as a star when she heard them begin to discuss something with what sounded like some urgency, Emin's voice rising in agitation. The truck slowed and then sped up again, and then slowed again before coming to a stop. She heard both of them get out and speak in muffled voices. A long moment of silence passed before she saw a reflection of light on the truck cab's rear window above her head. The only thing it could be would be the headlights of another vehicle approaching from the road behind them. She could hear the other vehicle now, its engine racing as it drew nearer. And then silence. A few seconds later, the stillness was shattered by the loud rattle of gunfire coming from beside the truck. She flinched and curled into a fetal position the best she could. More gunfire, this time from a distance away, the flat plunk of the rounds striking the bags of onions, and then came the deafening roar of an explosion.

25

The approach of nightfall, and what often seemed the mere pretense of a road, slowed their progress considerably. Gauging from their compass heading and the faint twinkle of lights on the western horizon, Masoud figured they were somewhere southwest of Mosul. According to the map, they would soon encounter an oil pipeline, and soon after that, the main highway. Reaching Bardarash meant taking a secondary road from there for perhaps seventy-five miles or so. Khalef had assumed the driving duties with Jihan riding shotgun. Before the darkness had fallen, they had all taken the time to lock and load their weapons in case they encountered the Turks along the way.

Masoud had been silent for most of the drive, as was Luke who periodically checked the bars on his phone. The batteries registered only ten percent. He couldn't afford any power usage until he knew for sure he might be able to reach Adele.

"I have given it much thought," Masoud said, breaking the silence. "The only thing that makes sense is that this Ozbek wishes to blame such an attack on Assad and the Syrians."

"On whose orders though?"

"Perhaps their president, Erdogan. He is a ruthless man. He has no love for we Kurds or Assad."

"Do you really believe Erdogan is foolish enough to approve of something like this? That would be a huge gamble to think no one would find out."

"Maybe it is someone else in their government. Or their military."

"Or Ozbek is just a rogue."

"What is rogue?"

"It is someone who is doing this on his own. By himself."

Masoud nodded. "Perhaps such a person is even more dangerous."

"Have you thought about what we do if we catch up to them? I mean he has my daughter with him. We can't just go at him shooting."

Masoud said nothing. Luke wondered if Maggie's wellbeing figured at all into Masoud's desire to stop Ozbek at all costs. He checked his phone again. Suddenly, there were three bars. He punched in Adele's number and waited. She answered after the first ring.

"Luke. Where are you?"

"Listen up, there's not much time. Where are you?"

"Duhok. But you need to know something."

"Adele, would you just listen?"

"Ozbek, His name is Ozbek, not Murat. He's Turkish military intelligence."

"I already know. I got your text."

"Where's Maggie?"

"I'm pretty sure he's got her with him."

"*Mein Gott!* Where are they?"

"Listen up. Ozbek is heading toward the UN refugee camp at Bardarash. We think he's going there to release Sarin gas. Wait…*Halte den Mund* for chrissakes! Just listen. You have to find some way to warn them, but you have to be careful. If Ozbek has her…" He faltered. "There may be a chance we'll catch up with him before he gets there, but if we don't, someone needs to warn them. Do you understand? You have to warn them. Tell them Ozbek's driving a white Mercedes four-wheel truck. Tell them about the Sarin."

"Where are you?"

"Somewhere on the back roads south of Mosul."

He felt Masoud touch his wrist. When Luke looked at him, Masoud was leaning over the seat and saying something to Khalef. "There," he said, turning to Luke. "You see? Tail lights. There. Ahead."

"Luke," Adele cut in. "Just promise me you'll get her back. Okay? We'll leave right away."

"Who's with you?"

"Harper. Harper Harris."

It took a few seconds for it to register. "Harper? How did…? Never mind. Hang on a second. We might've found them. The truck at least."

The tail lights looked to be a hundred yards or so ahead of them. The vehicle's brake lights flickered once, then twice, and then there was only darkness on the road ahead of them. Khalef slowed, approaching carefully. They could now see a truck about thirty yards ahead of them pulled to the side of the road and partially concealed by a clump of trees. It was a high-bed white truck of some sort. Luke couldn't tell for sure if it was the Mercedes.

Masoud said something to Khalef who abruptly stopped the SUV. He flicked on the SUV's fog lights in order to see the truck more clearly. Luke could just make out a figure standing at the edge of the light, cradling something in his arms. Before he could react, the windshield exploded. Luke instinctively ducked, fumbling for his rifle. Someone, Jihan, he realized, was returning fire from the cover of the open passenger side door. Masoud seemed to be still crouched behind the seat. Luke lifted his head just in time to see the man he had seen standing beside the truck raise something to his shoulder.

"RPG! Get out!" Luke yelled as he popped the door latch and slammed his shoulder against the door,

He must have instinctively grabbed Masoud's arm, yanking him along with him as they tumbled headlong onto the hard-packed road. Still gripping Masoud, Luke attempted to scramble away from the SUV just as the heat and concussion rolled him. It took what seemed an eternity for him to regain awareness of his surroundings. He raised his head and saw the SUV engulfed in flames. He yelled Masoud's name, but the sound seemed only to echo in his head.

Pushing up on all fours, he squinted through the thick smoke and saw what appeared to be a rolling jumble of flames some ten feet in front of him. It took him a couple of seconds to realize it was someone attempting to extinguish their flaming clothes. He scrambled to his feet, and upon reaching the flailing figure, he began slapping at the flames with his hands. In the light from the burning vehicle, he saw it was Jihan. In a matter of seconds, he managed to put out the flames. He pulled her to her feet and they stumbled a further ten yards or so from the burning hulk.

"Thank you," he thought he heard her say for he still couldn't hear very well.

Smoke curled from her still smoldering fatigue jacket, and her long black hair on one side of her head appeared singed close to her scalp.

"Are you alright?"

She had her hands on her thighs, coughing violently. "Yes," she said after a moment. "I think. Just my jacket. And hair," she said, touching the side of her head. She still clutched her rifle in her other hand. "Masoud. Where is Masoud?"

Luke turned, but didn't see any sign of the Kurd. He stumbled back to where they had landed and called Masoud's name. A faint voice answered from a clump of smoking brush beside the road. A moment later, Masoud lurched into the light, his one arm hanging limply at his side.

"Khalef," he said, his voice a hoarse croak.

Jihan had already circled around to the driver's side of the burning SUV. Luke could see her crouching as she approached the flaming inferno in an attempt to peer inside the vehicle. A moment later, she rejoined them. She shook her head.

"I saw him. I think they shot him… before." Her voice broke and she turned away.

Luke edged closer to the burning wreck and retrieved his rifle from where he had dropped it, and then walked a short distance up the road. He couldn't be sure due to the smoke and the darkness, but he couldn't see any sign of Ozbek's truck. They had gone. Maggie was gone. He had failed at the one task he couldn't allow himself to fail. He stood there a moment longer in stunned silence before turning back.

Jihan had stripped off her smoking fatigue jacket and was attempting to help Masoud to remove his own jacket when the roar of the flames was suddenly punctuated by the sound of the ammunition in the Land Cruiser exploding from the heat. They all three flinched and trotted a short distance down the road, not that it would help if a round went off in their direction. In the reflected light, Luke could see one side of Masoud's jacket was soaked in blood.

"How are you?"

Masoud gave a noncommittal shake of his head. "They are gone?"

"I'm afraid so." Luke walked towards the burning SUV as close as he dared, searching on the ground for his phone, but he didn't see it. He must've dropped it when they jumped out. He cursed in despair.

"Does anyone have a cell phone?" he asked, turning back.

Masoud gestured with his head that it was inside the SUV.

As long as there was still the slightest chance, he wouldn't quit, not yet. "How far is it to the highway to Mosul?"

"Ten kilometer maybe," Masoud said, wincing as Jihan finally managed to get his wounded arm out of his jacket.

Without hesitating, she stripped off her shirt, ripped off one sleeve and wrapped it around his upper arm. Then she fashioned for him a makeshift sling and helped him slip it on.

"Aren't you cold?" Luke asked, seeing that she now wore only a thin jersey.

"Kurdish women never complain about the cold," Masoud said. "They are like the animal. They do what they must," he said without amusement.

Jihan grunted in agreement and picked up her charred fatigue jacket from the ground and slipped it on.

"There must be a burial," Masoud said, staring at the burning wreckage. "But there is no time," he added as he dropped to his knees and slipped his wounded arm from the sling. Jihan joined him, kneeling beside him. They both raised their hands beside their heads, palms forward, and then leaned forwards, their heads almost touching the ground. They murmured what sounded like a prayer, finishing with a loud *Allahu Akbar,* and then rose to their feet.

"If we are fortunate we can find transportation at the highway," Masoud said. "If they have a phone, I shall call someone who may help."

"Who?"

Masoud didn't reply. Instead, he slung his coat over his good shoulder and started up the road.

26

"Luke! Luke!" Adele pulled the phone from her ear.

"What's going on?" Harper asked. She could hear the popping sounds coming from the phone from two feet away. "Is that someone shooting?"

Adele flinched as they both heard a loud banging sound.

"Luke! What is happening?" Adele shouted into the phone. "Don't hang up! Luke!" She quickly redialed his number.

Harper could tell from the look on Adele's face that Luke wasn't answering.

"What happened?"

"I don't know. The line is dead." She dialed again. "*Gott!*"

"What did he say?"

"He said they think they saw Ozbek's truck, and then… You heard it, too. Yes? It sounded like gunfire, and then an explosion."

"They were following Ozbek? Where were they? Adele, where were they?"

She looked at Harper, her face drained and expressionless. "Somewhere near Mosul," she said. "Luke said Ozbek was going to Bardarash. And something about him releasing Sarin gas. He thinks Ozbek has Maggie with him."

"Wait. Say that again. He's going to Bardarash to poison the camp? Are you sure?"

Adele appeared to be in a state of shock. "He has Maggie. Ozbek has Maggie," she repeated, her voice almost a whisper.

"We need to warn them."

Adele looked at her. "That was what Luke said."

"Call the police. Call someone. The Iraqi Police."

Adele sat there as if paralyzed.

"Give me your phone."

"Luke.... He is dead. You heard it. The explosion. Luke. Maggie. They are both gone. They have taken them both," she said, her voice devoid of emotion.

Harper wasn't sure what to say. Any reassurances would sound hollow. "Come on, Adele. Maggie may... Maggie is still alive. But we have to warn the camp."

Adele seemed to awaken from her fugue and looked at Harper. "And if we try to stop Ozbek? You know what will happen if someone tries to stop them."

"Adele. There are hundreds...thousands of lives at risk here. We have to tell someone."

"She is my daughter. I can't just...sacrifice her. That is what I would be doing."

Harper knew she was probably right. If anyone attempted to stop Ozbek by force, and if he had Maggie with him, it would surely end badly.

"Then we have to go there and warn them. Adele? Do you understand?"

Harper thought of something. "Hold on. I told you I've been to Bardarash." She pulled out her own cell phone from her daypack. "I might still have a cell number or at least the email address of the camp director. An Australian woman. Maybe I can reach her."

She opened her phone and began scrolling through the dozens of messages on her email. "Here it is. Shit! I thought she gave me her cell number.

All I've got is her email." She quickly typed in an email message asking Liz McDermott to call her back right away. It was an extreme emergency. Your camp is about to be attacked. She hit send.

"Let's go. Come on. Get dressed. Adele! We need to go!"

Adele looked at Harper. She almost appeared catatonic. "Yes," she said finally, gathering up her clothes and her handbag.

"I'll drive," Harper said.

Adele managed a thin smile. "You cannot be serious. You are a New Yorker. I am a German. I will drive."

Twenty minutes later, they arrived at the checkpoint marking the exit from Kurdish territory. Two bored looking uniformed policeman manned the barrier. Harper and Adele handed one of them their documents while the other guard circled their SUV.

"Where do you travel?" the one with their documents asked.

"Bar…" Adele started to say.

"Mosul," Harper quickly interjected. "The highway to Mosul is okay, yes?"

The policeman studied the documents for what seemed an interminable amount of time. "Yes, the road to Mosul is safe," he said, finally handing them back their papers.

As they drove off, Harper could see the other policeman talking to his partner and gesturing at the SUV's blown out rear window.

"We will have to take the same road we drove on this morning," Adele said. "You realize that, don't you?"

"I was afraid of that."

"It will be quicker. Perhaps less checkpoints."

Harper said nothing. Instead, she checked her phone again. There was still no reply from the McDermott woman at the camp. She felt reluctant to engage Adele in any conversation, afraid that the topic of Maggie's fate would only heighten Adele's obvious anxiety. And what happened to Luke? The whole situation seemed to have grown increasingly more perilous and uncertain. She tried to avoid thinking of the worst case scenarios. And what would they do once they reached the camp? What could they do? She only hoped the McDermott would call back and know what to do. They drove on into the darkness, each lost in their thoughts.

27

The night had grown increasingly colder, and occasionally a light drizzle mixed with sleet pelted their faces, stinging Luke's eyes and making it difficult to see in the dark. Twice, Masoud knelt in the muddy roadway in an attempt to determine if they were still following Ozbek's tire tracks. While confident they were on the right path, he also concluded that there was little sign of other recent tire tracks, thus lessening the chance they might encounter another passing truck, especially on a night such as this.

Luke regretted the fact he had left his seaman's cap and gloves in the Land Cruiser. The cold aggravated his burned hands, but not to the point where the pain diverted his attention from Maggie's dilemma. His experience as an infantry officer led him to always have a plan for a reasonable course of action. But he could come up with nothing. Outgunned, on foot, along with the fact that there were too many variables and unknowns, forced him to discard every option. All he could do was trudge onward, bent to the wind, and surrender to fate.

They had walked for perhaps an hour or more when they came upon the derelict burned out wreckages of three oil tanker trucks beside what appeared to be a well used macadam road. Seeing no other alternative, they followed the road northwards. After several minutes, they saw the road began to parallel a raised pipeline, and just visible in the distance, was the glow of lights. They quickened their pace the best they could in spite of their fatigue and Masoud's obvious pain.

After perhaps ten minutes, they came upon a tunnel beneath the roadway meant to allow vehicles to pass under the pipeline. The wind carried the sound of machinery, a generator from the sound of it. A moment later, they came over a slight rise and spotted a Quonset hut surrounded by a chain link fence and an array of bright security lights. The pipeline snaked through a tangle of smaller pipes inside the compound before doglegging to the north. A pumping station, Luke guessed, and better yet, one that seemed manned by someone gauging from the Jeep parked just outside the fence.

No sooner had they passed through the unlocked gate when someone emerged from the hut. The man, seemingly oblivious of their approach, began to climb onto a gangplank above the clot of pipes. They watched him for a moment as he, clipboard and flashlight in hand, went about his business inspecting the pipes. Masoud and Luke peered into one of the huts windows and saw a second man dozing at a desk. Masoud called out to the man on the gangplank, startling him to the point he almost fell off. A conversation ensued, and after a moment the man climbed down.

"Thanks be to Allah, this man is a Kurd," Masoud said. "He says he heard a truck pass by here less than an hour ago."

The man gestured for them to come inside. The hut was overheated and smelled of solvent and onions. Besides the lone desk, the only hint of habitation were a couple of cots, and a small cooking ring and a tea kettle.. The Kurd, a short, stocky man in thick, grease-stained overalls, launched into what seemed a longer than necessary narrative to his coworker, a grizzled, older man with a glass eye. As his colleague expounded, the other man's good eye veered back and forth from the bloodied Masoud to Luke's M-16 and then to Jihan's charred jacket.

As the Kurd spoke, he poured them each tea into tin cans that still bore labels advertising fava beans. After a minute or so of a one-sided and animated conversation, the Kurd turned to Masoud and offered him a cell phone. Masoud accepted it with a bow of his head, and then retrieved a small notepad from the pocket of his jacket. After finding what he wanted, he moved away from the others, and dialed a number. Whoever answered on the other end, seemed to listen in silence as Masoud spoke with hurried authority. Masoud fell silent for a minute before disconnecting. He started to hand the phone back to the Kurd and then handed it instead to Luke.

"You wish to call your friend?"

Luke had never told Masoud anything about Adele, but he had undoubtedly overheard their conversation in the SUV. Luke took the phone, dialed Adele's number, and waited as it went to voice mail. Why wasn't she answering? It wouldn't do any good to leave her this number, not unless they took the Kurd's phone with them. He was just about to offer the man two hundred dollars for his phone when Masoud interjected.

"He will drive us to the highway," Masoud said, slurping down the cup of tea. "A friend will meet us there, but we must hurry."

"Ask him if he will sell me his phone."

"There is no need. My friend will have a phone."

"I still think we should call someone. The police. The army. Someone."

Masoud seemed to consider this for a moment before replying. "It will do no good to call the police or the army. For even if they believe us, they will... What is the expression you Americans like to use? They will fuck it up, yes? If you must know, I called someone. A friend in the PKK. Now let us go."

"You told them about Maggie, right? That Ozbek has my daughter?"

Masoud patted Luke's shoulder assumingly. "We must go," he said and turned to the door.

28

Harper and Adele drove in silence, each reticent to share their thoughts. Every so often Adele began muttering something in German, the tempo of her soliloquy cascading into what could only be described as a rant. Sometimes, a stifled sob accompanied her ramblings. Once, Adele pulled abruptly to the side of the road, flung herself out and disappeared for five minutes. Harper heard her retching in the darkness, followed by a long silence before she returned. She said nothing as she swung back on the road, and resumed her maniac tempo, oblivious of the road conditions. A light rain had begun to fall soon after they left the Iraqi checkpoint, occasionally giving way to sleet. Adele drove on as if undeterred.

After a while, they came upon the small village where Adele had crashed into the HiLux. The truck sat abandoned beside the road. It was missing a rear wheel, and the axle was propped atop a pile of stacked flagstone.

"I guess they don't belong to Triple A," Harper said in an attempt at levity that she didn't really feel.

Adele stopped the Land Cruiser and stared at the HiLux for a moment before getting out.

"Where are you going?" Harper asked as Adele disappeared into the darkness.

A moment later, she reappeared carrying a large stone that she proceeded to heave through the truck's windshield. *"Zur Hölle mit ihnen,"* she muttered, climbing back in.

The village lie mostly in darkness, only two of the houses revealing dim light; the only visible inhabitants a pair of feral cats. Harper checked her phone again. Liz McDermott still hadn't replied. Was there a chance they were already too late? And then what? She didn't want to think about it. They drove on for several minutes before Adele broke the silence.

"*Wie machst Du das?*"

"For chrissakes, Adele. Speak English."

"I meant that I do not understand how you do this."

"Do what?"

"Deal with this… this shit."

"What shit?"

"The world's shit. *Der Weltschmerz*" Adele jerked the wheel as she crossed into the other lane to avoid hitting some small animal.

"Why don't you let me drive? You're going to get us killed."

Adele didn't reply.

"I told you. It's my job. I go where the stories are. The stories people need to know about. Jesus, I never realized how self-serving and lame that sounds."

"So in order to do that you must take photographs of the world's misery.

"And write about it. Look, believe it or not, I've done happy, feel good stories. Not a lot, but some."

"But this is what feeds you. Yes?"

"I learned it at my mother's knee. She had this old Brownie camera. She saved up for months to buy it at the Rich's department store in Atlanta. She liked to take pictures of the shanty towns, the broken down old farms, the people who grew up in slavery. She told me she didn't want anyone to ever forget. That's why I do it. So no one forgets."

"Do you still have them? Your mother's photographs?"

"No. They were lost when my mom's house burned down. But I can close my eyes and still see some of them. I didn't forget."

They again fell into a long silence. Fortunately, the rain had slowed to a steady drizzle, but still there were patches of fog in the low spots. The road was empty and dark with only the occasional abandoned farmhouse to break the monotony. Only once did they encounter another vehicle, a truck heading in the direction of Duhok.

"This is hopeless, you know," Adele said finally, her voice strained. "Luke is dead. And if Maggie is still alive, I fear she will not survive this night. And you and I? *Wir haben unsere Seelen in den Wind geworfen.*"

"Jesus, Adele. Stop it with this morose German bullshit. We need to think about what we're going to do."

"Why did you come with me?"

"You keep asking me that, and I keep telling you that I don't know. It's not just about a story. Not anymore. All I know is that I feel like I'm riding a log down a raging river and hanging on for dear life. Don't get me wrong. I've been in situations like this. It's just…I have a daughter now to consider."

Adele grunted but said nothing. Harper didn't want to admit to herself that if there was truly anything to this Sarin gas business, then there was indeed a story; a big one. A story that shouldn't be forgotten. If people only cared, she thought with more acceptance than bitterness.

"It was Luke's idea to break it off in Sarajevo. Not mine," she blurted out in some misguided attempt to change the subject. "I thought you should know that."

Adele looked at her, her face unreadable in the dim light of the dashboard. She shrugged. *"Alles ist vorbei. Weg.* I told you. Besides, it no longer makes any difference. Luke…" The words fell away.

They had been climbing a long hill, and as soon as they topped it, they saw the lights some fifty yards or so ahead. It took just a moment to tell the lights belonged to two parked vehicles that partially blocked the road. Adele slowed.

"What do you think?" she asked.

Harper could just now make out the two vehicles. One was a flat bed truck with high wooden sides, the other some kind of utility vehicle, like a Jeep, parked behind the truck. They slowed to a crawl some thirty yards away. The Jeep's headlights were trained on a line of a dozen or so people standing beside the truck; adults swathed in thick clothes, their gender indeterminable, and what looked to be several children.

"Shit," Harper cursed. "It's some kind of checkpoint."

They stopped ten yards away as a man wearing fatigues cautiously walked towards them, an automatic rifle slung over his shoulder. He wore some kind of a bandana around his head. A second man stood beside the Jeep. He also wore what someone might loosely consider a uniform, his military style fatigue cap his only nod to conformity. A third man, dressed similarly in fatigues, paced back and forth in front of the line of people standing beside the truck. He carried something long and thin in his hand, a cane perhaps. Suddenly, one of the people stumbled to their knees, and Harper saw the long thin object fall repeatedly onto the person's back. The figure crumbled onto the asphalt.

"My god! He's beating that man. This is not good." Harper glanced behind them. "Is there any way we can turn around?"

Adele didn't reply. The soldier with the bandana paused in front of their Land Cruiser as if he were inspecting their license plate. He craned his neck as he cautiously approached Adele's window. He pulled a small flashlight from his belt and shined it in Adele's face. Adele blocked the light with her hand as she rolled down her window. The man barked what sounded like a question. Harper caught a word or two. The Arabic word for what but that was all.

"Do you speak English?" Harper said, leaning across the seat.

The man looked to be quite young, no more than an adolescent. He glared at her and repeated the question. When neither of them answered, he spun on his heel and gestured for the man leaning on the Jeep to join him.

Adele reached behind Harper's seat and retrieved her handbag. "How much do we pay them?" she asked.

"Wait and see. Maybe this guy speaks English. They look like militia. PMG, probably. "

Harper could see that the third man, the one with the cane, was now holding a cloth bag in which the people beside the truck were tossing things. From what she could tell it appeared to be watches, jewelry, and wads of what looked like money.

"That asshole's robbing those people. They're probably refugees, and he's taking everything."

The second man consulted with the younger one and then approached Adele's window. He looked older but not by much, mid-twenties, maybe. His face reflected the spiteful look of testosterone induced bravado coupled with an over indulged sense of authority.

"Where do you go?" he asked in heavily accented English.

"We're going to Mosul," Harper said when Adele didn't answer.

"Your papers."

They each handed him their passports and visas. He studied them for a long moment in the beam of his flashlight. Harper had the impression the man couldn't read. He stepped in front of the Land Cruiser and bent at the waist to better study the papers in the headlights. His breath came out in small clouds of vapor as if the effort exerted him.

Meanwhile, the younger one circled the SUV. He hesitated as he stared at the blown out rear window before spending even more time inspecting the shattered side window. Then he went up to his partner who seemed to be still trying to decipher their passports. The younger one said something that made the other one straighten. The younger one pointed to the side window.

"I don't like this," Harper said,

Both of the militiamen turned their heads and stared at them through the windshield for a moment, before the older one reached into his pocket, retrieved a cell phone, and punched in a number.

"Shit, Adele!" She gripped Adele's hand. "They're going to know about yesterday."

"*Zur Hölle damit,*" Adele said, reaching into her handbag.

"Give him a hundred. Fuck, two hundred. Whatever it takes to get us out of here."

The militiaman spoke to someone briefly and then slipped the phone back into his pocket. He then said something to his comrade who began to walk off to join the third man who still seemed engaged in his petty larceny. As the militiaman approached Adele's window, she reached into the handbag and pulled out the Heckler.

"No! No! What in the hell are you doing?" Harper reached for Adele's wrist but she jerked free.

The militiaman yanked open Adele's door. "You come with us," he said, brusquely.

Before he could react, Adele jammed the automatic in the man's face. He jerked his head back, and Adele grabbed him by the collar of his fatigue jacket, the Heckler pressed into the man's cheek.

"Adele, don't."

"*Ich bin fertig mit diesedr sheiße!*" She looked at Harper. "I am done with all this. No more."

"Please, Adele."

She shoved the man backwards towards the Jeep, the handgun still pressed to his face. Only then did his companion turn and sense something was amiss. He started to unsling his rifle, but hesitated as Adele pointed the handgun at him. The other man holding the bag, now aware of what was happening, dropped the bag and started to reach for his sidearm.

"*Tu es nicht!*" Adele yelled, swinging the Heckler in his direction.

He started to pull out his handgun, and Adele shot him twice in the chest. One of the women refugees started to scream which set off a chorus of wailing from the children. Harper scrambled out of the SUV and ran up to Adele.

"What are you doing? Are you crazy?"

"On your knees," Adele ordered the other man who crouched in front of her. "Both of you. Tell him! On your knees! Both of you!"

The militiaman said something to the younger one who carefully slipped his rifle off his shoulder, and laid it on the ground before dropping to his knees. Just then, a band of sleet swept across the road, eliciting a murmur of discomfort among the refugees.

"Tell them to leave," Adele said to Harper. "The refugees. Tell them to leave."

Harper was too stunned to object. She walked over to the refugees who had huddled in a tight knot, the children shielded behind their backs. Harper could see their faces more clearly now. There were several old men, their ragged clothes mud stained and soaked. The women all wore threadbare woolen *hijabs* wrapped around their heads. She stared at them for a moment.

"Does anyone speak English?" she asked. She repeated the question a second time and a woman separated from the huddled figures.

"I speak English. A little." The woman sounded young, but Harper couldn't make out anything of her face beneath her *hijab*.

"Where are you going?"

"We go to the camp at Bardarash," the woman replied.

"Do not go there. Not tonight. It is not safe. Go on to Erbil. Do you understand?"

The woman nodded but didn't move as if waiting further instruction.

"Go! Now! To Erbil, not Bardarash. Do not go to the camp."

The woman turned and began speaking to her companions who seemed to make no effort to remount their truck. Of course, the bag of their belongings, Harper thought. She picked it up from the muddy asphalt and handed it to the woman. She nodded her thanks and then joined the others who had started to climb back onto the truck bed.

Harper looked down at the militiaman lying in the road. The rounds had hit him dead center in the chest. A faint cloud of vapor wafted up from the bloody wounds. Still gripped in the dead man's left hand was a three foot length of steel rebar. She allowed herself a twinge of satisfaction.

"Check them both for cell phones and bring their weapons," Adele shouted over the pelting of the sleet on the pavement.

Harper leaned down and pried the handgun from the dead man's hand and searched his pockets. She couldn't find a phone, only a pocket sized copy of what looked to be a prayer book, the Koran perhaps. The younger militiaman's phone was in his back pocket. She picked up his rifle and walked back over to Adele.

"You should go with them," Adele said, nodding at the truck. "This no longer concerns you. Here are your papers," she said, handing Harper her passport.

"The hell it doesn't concerns me. After what you just did? They'll look for us after this. Don't you get that?"

"We will be fine. They cannot report us. We have their phones."

"You don't understand. They'll figure this out. How hard do you think it's going to be for them to track down the Land Cruiser? A dead militiaman. Christ." She grabbed Adele's arm and jerked her around. "And what about them? Are you going to shoot them, too? They know what you did."

The militiaman kneeling at Adele's feet turned and looked at them.

"I told you. I no longer care," Adel said, staring down at the man kneeling in front of her. She looked up at the sound of the refugee's truck starting off. They both watched as it disappeared into the night.

"We should go, too" Harper said, trying to conceal the desperation in her voice.

Adele wiped the frozen rain from her face. "Very well. Do you know how to use that?" she asked, pointing at the gun in Harper's hand.

She had forgotten she still held it. "Yeah, I know how to use it."

"Watch them."

Adele walked over to the Jeep and fired a round into the front and rear tires. She then leaned into the cab and appeared to be searching for something. She turned and held up a cell phone and another rifle. Then she shot out the Jeep's headlights. She came back and gestured for the two soldiers to get up. The younger one lowered his head and began chanting what sounded like a prayer. She grabbed him by the collar and dragged him to his feet, shoving him over to his companion.

"Take your friend and get him off the road," she said to the one who spoke English. "Now!" She turned and looked at Harper. "Take the weapons and the phones and get in the car."

"Adele. What are you doing?"

The sleet had suddenly stopped, replaced by a thick mist that transformed the scene into a gauzy, surreal tableau of menace and even greater despair. Harper stood there a moment before picking up the weapons and phones.

"Let's go, Adele."

Adele looked at her. "Go to the car."

"Adele. Think about what you're doing."

"I am simply doing what must be done. Now go to the car."

Harper shook her head in dismay and started to walk to the SUV, and then turned. The two men had dragged their companion's body to the edge of the road. Adele said something, and they rolled it into the ditch. Adele looked back at Harper for a moment and then gestured to the two men to walk. It took just a few seconds for the three of them to disappear into the darkness beyond the SUV's headlights. A moment passed before she heard the three shots; two close together and few seconds later, the third. Adele emerged from the darkness, the Heckler held loosely at her side. She walked to the SUV without looking at Harper and climbed in. Harper waited a moment and then joined her. Adele sat staring straight ahead through the rain streaked windshield.

"Did you kill them?"

Adele looked at her. "You were right. They will find us. No, I didn't kill them," she added after a few seconds passed. "I told them to run."

"I'm not sure I believe you."

Adele shrugged. "Will this be in your story?"

"Jesus, Adele. You shot them, didn't you?"

Adele didn't say anything. Instead, she slipped the Land Cruiser into gear and pulled back onto the road.

29

Maggie lifted her head and glanced out the truck's window. The sleet had given way to drumming rain that for the moment had stopped. She twisted onto her side and flexed her legs. Emin…Murat turned to look at her. Neither he nor Hassan had said more than two words since they had stopped to place her in the truck's cab. Her legs had become so numb from the cold and lack of movement that Emin found it necessary to lift and carry her out of the truck bed. He slung her into the small backseat and tied her wrist restraints to the courtesy handle above the door. Even in the heated cab, her feet still felt numb. Her wet clothes didn't help matters.

"What are you doing, Emin?" she said as calmly as she could. When he didn't reply, she sat up and tried to lean forward. "I guess you didn't want me to freeze to death. Is that it? It must be because of those warm fuzzy feelings you still have for me."

He didn't take the bait, and instead began talking with Hassan. She was sure of it now. They were speaking in Arabic. She thought she heard the word Bardarash, and she remembered Emin promising her they would be visiting the camp at Bardarash. It was all still bewildering. Why did they want to go to the camp? Whatever he had in mind couldn't possibly be anything legitimate, much less benign. So why? All she knew was that she was afraid.

"Who were the people shooting at us?" she asked.

"It is not your concern. Besides, they are no more."

She kicked her legs against the back of his seat in some helpless fit of defiance. Emin leaned over the seat and grabbed her leg.

"Stop! Or I will put you back out."

When she kicked at him, he started to raise his hand and then stopped. Instead, he reached onto the floorboard behind his seat and carefully lifted up a backpack stowed there. Something in his demeanor telegraphed apprehension, fear even. He held the pack as far away from him as possible as he carefully placed it on the floorboard between his legs. He turned again and looked at her.

"*Ne ekersen, onu bicersin,*" he said with sort of a mocking gravity. "It is a saying amongst my people. Yours, too, I believe. You will reap what you sow. You will soon reap. I am truly sorry that it is you that must be involved in this. You seemed like such a nice young woman," he said with a hint of sarcasm. "You would have perhaps made a good wife. If one could forget you are a whore like all Western women."

"Fuck you, Murat."

"Emin.

"Fuck you, Emin."

"We are almost there. Then your suffering will be over." He nodded and turned back in his seat.

She wriggled her fingers in an attempt to get some feeling back into them. The restraints were still wet and slick. Maybe she could slip them off. She kept her eyes on the back of their heads and began twisting her wrist. She figured she didn't have much time. And if she managed to get her hands free, then what? Open the door and jump? If she survived the fall, they would undoubtedly find her. She briefly entertained the fantasy of reaching over the seat and clawing out Hassan's eyes. It might cause them to wreck. Then all bets would be off. She had to do something, she thought as she kept wriggling her wrists.

A half hour passed, and to her dismay, the restraints felt no looser. Soon, they passed a road sign announcing Bardarash 2km. And then a sign that had the words UNHCR painted in large blue lettering, and below that something printed in Arabic and another language she didn't recognize. Emin said something to Hassan who cut the headlights and drove slowly for another half minute or so before stopping. Emin picked up a pair of binoculars and began scanning the road ahead.

Maggie raised her head. She could make out some lights ahead of them. An array of bright lights illuminating what looked like a cluster of double–wide trailers. It had to be the camp, she thought, settling back down. Emin lowered the binoculars and muttered what sounded like a curse. He said something to Hassan who carefully backed up, turned the truck around and drove back the way they had come, still without the headlights. They drove like this for a half-minute or so before Hassan turned the headlights back on and turned off the road.

The truck rocked back and forth as they drove over the rough terrain. At one point, Maggie sensed they were driving up a steep incline. She lifted her head again to look over the seat. They seemed to have stopped atop a small hill overlooking a rectangle of lights surrounded by darkness. Inside the rectangle, were more lights, though faint and scattered. It had to be the camp.

The two men climbed out and carefully closed the doors. She could hear them talking, their conversation interrupted by long silences. Then she heard the sound of someone rifling through the crates on the back of the truck. Another five minutes of muted conversation before Emin climbed back in the truck.

"What are you doing, Emin?"

He started to say something, and then hesitated. "I am changing history," he said quietly. "Who amongst us has not wanted to do that?" He opened the glove box and removed something and turned and looked at her. "Let us now go and sign our names in the book of history."

Dennis Jung

Emin climbed out of the truck and stood there a moment alone, staring down at the camp. The wind at his back gusted and then settled to a stiff, steady breeze. He could smell the approaching rain, and it reminded him of the winters of his childhood in the small village on the slopes of Ararat. He could still remember being forced by his stepfather to walk many miles to gather wood, and the beatings when he returned with no more than bundle of twigs. His was not a happy childhood. The man in Istanbul who had recruited him, a military officer of uncertain rank, told him this was a valuable attribute for someone performing the job for which they were recruiting him. That and a sense of patriotism, he added. We will provide all else that is needed, the officer assured him. Emin wasn't even his given name. Neither was Murat, nor Nabil, nor a half-dozen other names.

Hassan would have by now reached the camp perimeter. Emin would allow him a few more minutes in case he had to cut through the fence. He had needed to instruct Hassan twice on how to arm the timers on the three small packs of explosives. And still the ignorant dolt seemed unsure. He reminded him also of the need to wear the gas mask, not that it would help, for Emin had removed the mask's filters that morning. In any event, Hassan wasn't wearing the proper protective clothes anyway. He was meant to be expendable; a Syrian provocateur. A terrorist with a Syrian passport sewn into the lining of his knapsack.

He raised the binoculars and trained them on the gate. There was more security than he had anticipated. Several SUVs sat parked just inside the gates. He counted a half-dozen or more men loitering beside one of the trailers. All armed from what he could tell. They were likely others patrolling the perimeter. Had they somehow been alerted? But how? Other than the brief skirmish on the road with the militia, their journey had been uneventful.

He lowered the binoculars and winced at the pain in his forearm. He thought of Maggie then and his dilemma of what to do with her. She knew too much, not so much as to focus blame, but still…. Hassan's Syrian passport and the military backpacks with the Syrian Army insignia would

206

certainly lay the blame at the bastard Assad's feet. But yet he knew he could not leave Maggie behind to tell her tale. He stepped into the protective overalls, zipped them up, and then picked up the mask and the backpack and strode back to the truck.

30

"Bloody hell! You're going to make me break my rule about drinking after nine," Liz McDermott muttered and leaned down to open her desk cabinet. She looked up at them each in turn. "Either of you care to join me?"

Harper held up her thumb and index finger an inch and a half apart. Adele said nothing, instead she sat there, stone-faced and for once subdued, McDermott removed what looked to be a half-gallon size bottle of Beefeaters from the cabinet and heaved it onto the desk.

"You'll have to find your own glass, Miss Harris. Try over there," she said, nodding at a nearby desk. "You were just here, weren't you? Five months ago, was it?" she asked, filling what seemed half of her coffee cup.

"Six," Harper said, grabbing an empty cup from the desk. She sniffed it and held it out to McDermott who sloshed in more like three fingers worth. "Listen. There may not be much time. You must have some kind of plan for things like this?"

"What? A plan for a nerve gas attack?" She snorted. "If you're wondering if we have an evacuation plan. Sure, I have one. And according to the best estimate it will take two days to clear the camp. Is that enough time? I didn't think so," she said in response to Harper's look of dismay. "I suppose mass panic will have to do. Before I go yanking the alarms please assure me you are right about this?" she said, turning to look at Adele.

"I told you what Luke said. He didn't have time to provide details, just that there might be a Sarin attack at this camp," Adele said, her voice without emotion,

"Might be, did you say?"

"No, he said…. Look, we have told you all we know."

"It's just that I will have to notify someone. The Iraqi National Police. I would be derelict in my duties if I didn't. But I don't want to go into that half-cocked. The truth is we don't have the best relationship with the police. In fact, it's unlikely they will respond. For one, they don't like the refugees, and the last time I called them to put down a food riot their men ended up getting stoned and one of their vehicles was set afire."

"So an evacuation is out of the question?" Harper asked for the second time.

"Entirely out of the question." She looked back at Adele. "Did your husband mention that he was here several days ago?"

"Ex-husband. And yes, he said something about coming here."

"He came to look for your daughter. I'm guessing she is somehow involved in this?"

"They have her. They abducted her. And I…" Adele looked away for a moment before taking a deep breath. "If they have her, any effort to intercept them… to attack them, and my daughter will most likely die."

"So why did they bring her along?"

"They are using her for something. To get in the camp. A Trojan Horse. I don't know." Adele lowered her head and rubbed her eyes. "Either way, it will not end well for her." She raised her head and looked at Harper.

No one said anything for a long moment. "So what do we do?" Harper asked.

"I have two well-armed gate guards, and two more people that are little more than night watchmen. One of them guards the supply compound, and the other patrols the camp. He's not even armed. I have my admin people and some aid workers, a doctor and two nurses and a medic. A dozen and a half hands in all."

Harper looked at Adele. "What do you know about Sarin?"

Adele broke from her distraction and sat up. "It is quite nasty and lethal in even very minute amounts. Death is fairly rapid and usually due to muscle paralysis, inability to breathe. It can be dispersed by bombs, aerosol, put in a water supply. There is an antidote. Atropine. You don't happen to have several thousand or so doses on hand, do you?"

"I have to report this," McDermott said, reaching for her phone. "I'm sorry," she said to Adele. "but if I don't then…"

There was a sudden knock on the door and one of the gate guards came in. "There is someone at the gate. They say they have come to help us."

"Who is it?"

The guard shrugged and cocked his head. McDermott took a swallow of her vodka, grabbed her jacket and started for the door. Harper and Adele looked at each other and then followed after her.

Since their arrival at the camp, the wind had picked up, the gusts filling the air with swirls of light drizzle. The mist and the low hanging clouds lent a sickly yellowish glow to the illumination cast by the half-dozen or so halogen lights marking the camp's entrance. Harper could make out three vehicles, a couple of SUVs and three pickup trucks lined up just outside the gate. A couple of figures stood in the headlights of the SUV, their shoulders hunched into the wind.

Harper and Adele hurried to maintain stride with McDermott who marched stiffly yet resolutely toward the gate. The two figures on the other side of the gate moved forward in anticipation as the guard swung open the gate. Harper could see one of them wore some sort of head covering that revealed only a bearded face. The man shuffled rather stiffly through the gate.

The other man was taller and wore a down jacket, his head bare. Something about the man's posture and stride tugged at her memory.

She realized then it was Luke. She was sure of it. Adele must have recognized him also, for she first came to an abrupt halt, and then hurried forward, brushing past McDermott. She stood before Luke for a moment and said something to him that Harper couldn't catch in the howling wind. They embraced; a tentative, uncomfortable attempt to hug at first, then Adele clung to him with obvious desperation. Harper stopped a good ten feet away and watched. Luke seemed to stare over Adele's shoulder at Harper for a moment before breaking free and turning to McDermott.

"We need to talk," Luke shouted over the sound of the wind and the growling SUV engines. He drew Masoud closer. "This is Masoud. He and his friends are here to help. Can we come in?"

McDermott nodded and gestured to the guard to open the gate, and then turned and started back to the trailer. Luke and Adele and the man called Masoud started to follow her. Harper stood and waited until Luke drew near. He and Adele stopped in front of her. Adele hesitated and then broke away and followed McDermott.

"Harper," he said.

Harper nodded. They both stood there, immobilized by their discomfort before Harper lifted her arms in a gesture more of uncertainty than greeting. The sudden swirl of emotions left her at a loss for words. He responded by also raising his arms. She waded into his embrace with an awkwardness commiserate to time and circumstance.

"I never expected to see you again. At least, not like this," he said, clutching her and leaning into her ear in order to be heard above the gusting wind.

"Likewise." She pulled away and looked at him. "We both thought you were dead."

"Nine lives and all that shit. How are you?" He laughed with the same baritone hoot that could be either annoying or amusing depending on the circumstances. "That suddenly sounds very superficial under the circumstances. But I guess I need to know."

"Do you mean how do I feel right now or how have I been since we last saw each other?"

"Right now. The rest will have to wait."

"It's been a ride. With Adele, I mean. She's a…"

"A force of nature."

Harper considered whether she should reveal the incident on the road. This wasn't the time, she decided. "Let's just say they're probably printing the wanted posters as we speak."

"That bad?"

"Like you said, the rest will have to wait. We should go in."

McDermott had removed the Beefeater from her desk and replaced it with a coffee maker. As she filled it, she shifted her glance to Masoud and then to Luke. "Who are your friends?"

Luke looked at Masoud before answering. "PKK."

"Wonderful. If the Iraqis find out I allowed PKK into the camp they'll shut us down for sure."

"Do they know about this?"

"The police? I was just about to call them when you showed up."

"Then I'd hold off until we know more about what's happening."

"So what is happening?"

"All we were told us was they were going to Bardarash to gas the camp. They might have plastic explosives. If so, they may be going to disperse it with a bomb. Maybe on a timer."

"Or in a suicide vest," Harper added half-aloud.

"Yeah, that's a possibility. Either way, we're grasping at straws in the dark. We managed to catch up with them on the road a little after sundown. It didn't end well for our side. If they're coming here tonight, then the chances are they're already here and are just waiting somewhere out there."

"They are watching. And waiting," Masoud offered from where he leaned on the wall.

Harper noticed the man's bloody sling for the first time, as did McDermott.

"Do you need medical assistance? We have a doctor on duty," McDermott asked.

Masoud shook his head. "It is nothing. If he watches, than perhaps he saw our arrival."

"We're pretty sure there are only two of them," Luke added.

"And you think they will sneak into the camp? Infiltrate?" McDermott asked.

"Perhaps," Masoud replied. "They will not come through the gate."

"Is the camp fenced?" Luke asked.

"Only parts of it. There are more unfenced areas than I care to mention. You might as well assume the perimeter is largely insecure. I told them earlier, we have a night watchman out there carrying nothing more dangerous than a flashlight and a cell phone."

"For all we know, they could be out there right now dispersing the gas," Adele said, breaking her silence.

"Christ," McDermott said, holding her hands to her face.

"Then our only choice is for us to find them first," Luke said."Do you have any gas masks?"

"The last inventory I saw showed twenty of them. They're kept in that Quonset hut. By the shed where we were the other day," she said, glancing at Luke. "Just don't ask me which pile of supplies they're under."

Luke looked at Masoud. "What do you think?"

"I will send some of the men to search outside. The truck may be near."

"And if they find the truck and they are not there?"

Masoud thought. "Then we must search the camp."

Everyone fell silent as they pondered the implication of what Masoud had just suggested.

"I guess we don't have any choice," Luke said finally. He turned to Masoud. "Okay. Send out some of your men." Luke shot Adele a glance before placing his hand on Masoud's shoulder. "Tell them that they have my daughter. You need to tell them that."

"I understand. I will go with them, my friend."

"Thanks. I'll check out the camp. Do you think any of your men would volunteer to go with me? They need to know about the gas though."

Masoud nodded. "Take Jihan. You may need a translator. I will talk to her," he said and walked out.

"How badly is he wounded?" McDermott asked.

"He won't say. Do you have an extra cell phone I could use?"

"Sure." She reached into her desk and brought one out. "My number's saved under contacts."

Luke looked at Adele. "You and Harper stay here. I'll call if I find anything."

"I'll go with you," Adele said.

"No. You're staying. Just for once, listen to me!" he said with a flash of anger. "If..." He stopped himself.

"If I would have just stopped her. Is that what you were going to say?"

"No, that wasn't what I was going to say. I was going to say if things go to shit, then one of us should be here. For Maggie. Just stay. Okay?"

Adele didn't reply.

"Coffee anyone? Vodka?" McDermott asked in an attempt to defuse the obvious tension between them.

"I need a flashlight and a map if you have one."

"I can make you a copy."

"I'll be right back," Luke said and left without so much as a glance at Adele or Harper.

31

Masoud and Jihan were waiting at the gate. Masoud handed Luke a Glock and an M-16. "And this," he said pulling something from beneath his jacket. "You may need."

Luke saw it was a pair of night vision glasses. He looked at Jihan. "You understand what we're doing?"

She nodded. "What are we looking for?"

Jihan's directness and aptitude continued to impress him, for she obviously knew to ask the right questions.

"I would say we're looking for two men. Maybe just one. Young. Old? I don't know, but they're probably carrying a backpack and looking suspicious. Do you know what I mean?"

"Suspicious. Sneaky? Like Wiley Coyote?"

Luke shook his head in amusement. "The Roadrunner cartoons. I forgot you used to watch them."

"And if I see him? This coyote?"

"Do what you think is right. Just remember he will have the gas with him. If you think he's already released it, shoot him and leave quickly."

She nodded again, this time with an exaggerated somberness.

"Wait here," he said and turned back to the double wide.

McDermott was holding her cell phone to her ear and drumming the desk with her fingers. Harper sat on the edge of the desk, studying a piece of paper that he could see looked like a map. Adele was nowhere to be seen.

"Where's Adele?"

"She just went out to see you. Not more than a minute ago."

He shook his head in irritation. "When she comes back, tell her to stay put."

McDermott lowered the phone. "My night watchman doesn't answer. Sometimes that's not unusual." She took the map from Harper and handed it to him. "Here is this and a pair of lamps," she said, passing him a pair of military grade mini-flashlights "Good luck, Luke. Call in if you find anything. I hate to say it, but we may need a running start."

"You won't try to evacuate the place?"

"To what end? It would probably create a panic we couldn't contain. At this point, we can only pray and hope you can find and stop them in time."

Luke turned for the door, nodded to Harper and then hesitated. He wanted more than anything to talk to her, be with her, even if just for a few minutes. "We…" he started. "I'll be back," was he all he managed to come up with. It would have to wait.

"Be careful," she said as she slipped out the door.

Jihan was waiting outside the trailer. He handed her a flashlight and turned his on and held the map up against the wall of the trailer. "So we are here." He traced with his finger a route that circumvented the north side of the camp. He figured with the north wind at their backs someone releasing a canister of gas would approach from the north and hope the wind would carry the gas into the camp. It would be safer for them.. And for us, too, Luke thought. "If we don't find them then we go into the camp."

They cut through a row of half-dozen or so double wide trailers. The barracks for the camp's aid workers, Luke guessed, gauging from the animated voices overlapping muted music. It reminded him of the long evenings spent in the bunkers after missions, though more often than not the music was the lament of the latest country music ingénue, and the conversations were invariably fueled by contraband mini-bottles of bourbon. The wind had grown colder, the clouds lower, and he felt an occasional drop of moisture pelt his face.

He illuminated his watch to check the compass bearing before leading Jihan through a row of tents. Most had the tent flap that served as the doorway tied back revealing dim scenes of domestic activity; women cooking on small portable stoves, the children huddled around them, their faces illuminated only by the flames. After passing several of them, Jihan broke away when they passed a tent with a handful of children standing in the opening. Jihan went to the tent and appeared to have a conversation with someone inside.

"What?" he asked when she rejoined him.

"I told them to bring the children inside and fasten their tent tightly."

Luke said nothing. What could he say? This might all become an exercise of futility, and a fatal futility at that. They moved on, not stopping until they reached the last row of tents. Luke put on the night vision goggles, adjusted them, and then scanned the slope that swept up to what the map showed was the fenced perimeter. Nothing moved. The Quonset supply hut where McDermott had brought him to view the young woman's body sat separate from the tents, perhaps a hundred yards or so away and along the bottom of the slope. That afternoon at the shed seemed longer ago than just a couple of days. He wondered if she was buried somewhere along the slope. He also wondered of anyone had asked about her. He gestured to Jihan to follow him.

They had traversed the slope perhaps halfway when they almost stumbled on the body sprawled in a slight depression. Luke crouched beside it, and shielding his light, shone it on the face of a grizzled older man wearing a threadbare fatigue jacket and muddy insulated pants. Someone had cut his throat. It was most likely the body of the watchman who wasn't answering his phone. He glanced at Jihan, and guessing from the look on her face, she had reached the same conclusion.

He led them higher up the slope in order to get a better sense of the camp's layout. Gauging by the direction of the wind and the location of the watchman's body, he figured whomever was going to release the gas would follow this slope down from here towards the camp. At this point, he had no way of knowing if there was more than one of them, or if they had taken Maggie with them.

He raised the goggles and scanned the slope. A small knoll rose a short distance away. There appeared to be a clump of low growing trees marking the summit. If nothing else, it would provide them some cover as they scanned the camp below them. It had started to sleet again, a slow drizzle at first, and then swells of icy, wind-driven squalls that required them to push forward with their shoulders hunched and faces turned. The night vision goggles were suddenly useless.

"Take these," he said, handing the goggles to Jihan. "Go along the ridge. If you see someone, shoot them. Just remember they have my daughter. Understand? And if you hear an explosion, you run. Run into the wind."

She nodded and stood there as if awaiting some further instruction.

"I am going down into the camp. So be careful you don't shoot me. Okay?"

She nodded again and disappeared into the darkness. Once in the trees, he saw that they sheltered a pile of rubble that might once have been a small stone hut, the remnant of its walls no higher than a foot or two.

All of his intuition told him they were running out of time. He had no choice but to take his chances and go into the camp. He reminded himself that if worse came to worse he still had the syringe of Atropine in his belt bag. Grim satisfaction, he thought in light of the consequences of failure.

He hunkered down below the wall out of the driving sleet and took out McDermott's cell phone. Because of his cold fingers, it took him what seemed forever to text his intention to go into the camp. For a fleeting moment, he considered texting Adele, but then realized he didn't have her number. There wasn't time anyway. This whole ordeal seemed to be nothing but misconnections. The story of my life, he thought bitterly. Misconnections; his father, then Harper. Adele. And now Maggie.

He stuffed the phone back into his pocket and slipped the M16 from his shoulder. Swiping the rain from his face, he pushed to his feet and started to step over the wall. He froze as a shape loomed out of the darkness no more than ten feet away. It couldn't be Jihan, he thought as he hesitated. He switched off the safety on the M16 and raised it to his hip as he flicked on the flashlight. The figure standing there wore a gas mask and carried a knapsack in one hand and something that looked like an Uzi in the other. Luke quickly switched off the light, firing at the same time. He didn't hear the answering volley, only felt the white hot pain searing his left arm and leg. He fell back, his leg crumpling beneath him.

It was suddenly silent. All he could hear was the ringing in his ears and his own grunt of pain. He waited a few seconds before dragging himself back to the wall, and then carefully raised his head over the parapet. The dim lights of the camp reflecting off the low clouds provided just enough light to see the silhouette of someone struggling to their knees.

Luke started to raise his rifle just as the figure hurled something towards him. It bounced off the wall in front of his face. A grenade? He frantically searched the ground in front of him.

Just then, a volley of shots rang out from his left, and the figure fell from sight. A second later, the explosion knocked him onto his back. He lay there too stunned to move. Again, there was only silence and the ringing in his ears. It took him just a moment to realize the wall had blocked most of the blast. He tried to sit up, but grimaced in pain. He realized then his left pant leg was soaked in blood.

"Luke!" someone shouted, the voice barely audible over the ringing in his ears. Then, a light shined in his face.

"Luke!"

"What? You can't be here."

Adele dropped to her knees beside him. "We need to go," she shouted, pulling him to his feet.

"Can't walk. My leg. You have to run."

There came the muffled sound of a second explosion from somewhere down the slope,

"Come on, Luke. Get up!"

She tried again to pull him to his feet, but he proved too heavy. As she collapsed atop him, he grunted in pain. Pulling himself from her embrace he fumbled for the belt bag. It seemed to take forever to unsnap it. He grasped the syringe with his stiff fingers, jammed the end of it between his teeth and pulled off the cap

"What are you doing?" she screamed as she struggled to clutch him to her.

He slammed the syringe into her arm. She winced and tried to pull away, but he held on until he thought the syringe was empty.

"*Nein! Nein! Was hast du gemacht?* What are you doing?" she yelled as she yanked the syringe from his grasp.

"There's gas. Other side of the wall."

He tried to raise his arm to point but it felt limp and useless. She pulled him against her chest, cradling his face tightly into the folds of her jacket as if it would somehow protect him. He felt her reach down and trace her fingers lightly over his face much as a blind person might. He held her hand to his mouth and rolled over and stared up at the drifting sleet.

32

He's dragging me like a sheep to slaughter, Maggie thought as she stumbled again on the steep rocky slope. She fell to her knees, and he jerked her back upright, the coarse rope burning into her neck. For some reason, he had untied her hands, only to replace the bindings with the noose round her neck. The cold rain had soaked her clothes, and despite the exertion of stumbling, falling, and trying to keep pace with Emin, she shivered violently from the cold as much as from her fear. She had long ago come to the realization that he was planning to kill her. Here on this cold barren slope or in the camp. Either way, it no longer made any difference.

At first, she guessed the shiny yellow overalls were meant to keep him dry. Then, out of a sense of absurd morbidity, she concluded the suit was meant to keep her blood from soiling his clothes. It was only after she brushed against him and felt the suit's stiff, impervious texture that she realized why he wore it. In that next instant, she recognized the bundle attached to his waist was a gas mask. He was going to gas the camp.

She stumbled again, and he stopped to look at her.

"Enough, Murat. I know what you're doing. Just kill me now," she gasped, clutching at the rope around her neck.

He seemed to consider her request for a moment before reaching into his day pack and removing a handgun. "It is your choice. I owe you that."

She pulled at the rope, forcing him to move closer. He raised the gun and held it to her forehead. The rattle of gunfire from somewhere just below made him hesitate and pull back. A moment passed, the only sound the pelting of the sleet on Emin's stiff yellow overalls. Then another volley of shots followed quickly by an explosion. She saw the flash of the detonation reflected off the low clouds. Emin stood still and silent, as if waiting. Another explosion, this time muffled and seemingly from farther down the slope in the direction of the camp.

Emin knelt and reached into the pack and retrieved a small bundle. All she could tell in the darkness was it appeared cylindrical. He appeared to do something with it before placing it on the ground beside him.

"It is time," he said and then muttered something. She heard the word Allah.

Yes, it was time, she thought. It's now or never. She reached into the pocket of her pants, her stiff fingers curling over the shard of glass. She grabbed the rope as she withdrew the shard, jerking him closer, throwing him off balance. As he tried to recover, she wrapped one arm around his neck to pull him to her, and then stabbed the shard into his throat.

He rocked back on his heels, and she sensed his surprise as he dropped the rope and clutched at his throat. She scrambled backwards on all fours and then turned and ran, stumbling and tripping on the slick stone, and running again. Lights. There were lights. She swiped her wet hair from her eyes. Lights and voices.

EPILOGUE

IRAQI REFUGEE CAMP ATTACKED WITH NERVE GAS

November 27th, 2019 - Baghdad (Al Jazeera) - Sources in the Iraqi government have confirmed reports that the Bardarash refugee camp in northern Iraq was attacked two nights ago by at least two assailants whose intention had purportedly been to release Sarin gas in the confines of the camp. The resulting casualties consisted of fifteen refugees, mostly women and children, a security guard, and three aid workers. General Amir Hasan, the head of the Iraqi National Police, stated the death toll would have been far higher were it not for the heavy wind and rain that struck the camp at the time of the attack and hindered the gas' dispersal.

Sarin is a particularly lethal nerve gas that is considered a weapon of mass destruction and its production and stockpiling has been banned since 1997. In spite of the ban, there have been at least a half-dozen investigated instances of its use against civilians over the past seven years. All of these past attacks were purportedly initiated by the Syrian military, an accusation disputed by spokesmen for Syrian President Bashar al-Assad. The most notorious incident being the attack on Ghouta in which various sources placed the death toll in the range of 300 to as high as 1700 people.

As of this reporting, the Iraqi government has declined to confirm either the identity of the two dead terrorists, or if their investigation has identified the attack's sponsor. Also, no group has yet come forward claiming responsibility for the attack, although unconfirmed suspicions all indicate one of several Syrian government allied factions as the likely perpetrator.

TURKISH BORDER, DUHOK GOVERNORATE, KURDISTAN NOVEMBER 27TH

Harper wrapped the coarse woolen muffler more tightly around her neck before tugging open the crude wooden door. For a moment, she stood stooped over inside the low threshold so as to savor the crisp mountain air, a sharp contrast to the smoky confines of the tiny alcove where she had slept. She stepped out onto the slab of stone that served as the porch and saw for the first time the village where they had sought refuge. Ever the photographer, she allowed her eyes to survey the landscape before her, taking in the light and shadows that sketched the low stone and adobe houses, weighing the close shot as opposed to a wide angle, mentally cropping the images where needed.

She never caught the name of the village, and was told only that from time immemorial its isolation and proximity to the Turkish border cemented its reputation as a prime smuggling wayside. The Kurd named Masoud had informed them that the dwelling where they had sought shelter was ostentatious by the standards of the surrounding village, for it had once belonged to the village grocer and mayor. Obviously, such a level of gentry required what Architectural Digest might graciously describe as an open floor plan living space. The mayor had opted for the Kurdish equivalent of a small two bedroom ranch style with a compact kitchen, the bedrooms the size of closets, and an absence of indoor plumbing. The wealth of a grocer in a small mountain village apparently had its limits.

All of this had been related to them by Masoud while he supervised the preparation of the previous night's meal by an old woman who grunted in agreement at certain salient points during Masoud's narrative, her lack of English seemingly not a barrier. The meal had been simple but satisfying, goat stew and fresh flat bread. Harper had perched on a stool and watched the old woman slapping the dough between her palms before tossing it onto a hot griddle. It brought to mind a long forgotten memory of her mother frying corn cakes in much the same manner.

They had arrived soon after dark, thus preventing Harper from gaining much of an appreciation of their surroundings. Now as she studied the village in the bright morning sunlight, she had the odd sense of déjà vu. The flat sloping rooftops at once reminded her of a hillside settlement on the Moroccan-Algerian frontier that she had photographed for National Geographic. Something about this village's seclusion and how it blended into the surrounding hills called to mind a similar village in the Guatemalan highlands that housed refugees fleeing their government's predations. All such places seemed to smell the same; wood smoke and animal dung and something indefinable but yet pleasantly exotic.

The vista made her regret having abandoned her camera along with her luggage in the hotel room in Duhok. They had dared not go back to reclaim their things after learning the Iraqi National Police had already been to the hotel searching for them. This information had been gleaned from a report obtained by a PKK informant in the Mosul Police headquarters. This also meant foregoing any flight out of Baghdad. Hence, here they were awaiting a covert overnight passage across the Turkish border.

She gave the mud and stone houses their due before lifting her eyes to take in the surrounding hillside and the snow covered mountains looming just beyond. The snow storm of two days ago had obviously blanketed the area quite heavily, rendering the narrow rutted track leading to the village almost impassable. Twice, the driver and Masoud were forced to jam stones beneath the wheels to gain sufficient traction.

Shielding her eyes from the glare, she squinted to see if she could see where Adele and Maggie might have gone. An hour or so earlier, she heard them from the sanctuary of her alcove as they attempted to slip quietly out through the creaky door. It didn't surprise her that they chose not to announce their departure or its purpose. Neither Adele nor Maggie had spoken much on the drive to the village. Harper sensed their silence stemmed from grief as much as exhaustion. She too felt numb and battered by the events of the last several days.

Tomorrow evening they would be in Istanbul, the day after that somewhere in a European stopover. And then home. It never ceased to amaze her how modern travel allowed one to journey from a remote mountain village such as this to her Brooklyn flat in a matter of a couple of days journey. What she found even more remarkable was the fact she had left New York a mere four days ago. So much had transpired in that span of time.

The last thirty-six hours had been especially arduous. It had started in the rush of confusion at the camp; the muffled explosions and gunfire, the headlong flight into the darkness as Liz McDermott attempted to shepherd as many refugees as possible out of harm's way. It was there on the road in the mass of panicked refugees that Masoud and his men appeared with Maggie in tow. In the midst of this chaos, Adele remained missing, even her disappearance the previous night still a mystery.

It wasn't until almost two hours later that Adele appeared at the gate. By then, the Iraqi police had arrived, further adding to the confusion and mayhem. Harper had watched Adele and Maggie's reunion from a distance, but was still able to witness their sudden groundswell of grief. Maggie collapsed in her mother's arms, her shrieks and wails overshadowing the shouting of the terrified refugees.

Harper had lingered at a distance, partially out of respect for their privacy and partially out of her own grief and sense of helplessness. The sketchy details of Luke's death only made it even so much more difficult. Even after the camp had been cleared the following morning, the details of what had occurred remained unclear. Adele, still in a state of shock, couldn't or wouldn't shed light on whether Luke had succumbed from his wounds or the gas, only that he had died while trying to protect the camp.

A cursory medical examination that morning suggested that Adele had been exposed to the Sarin, but had somehow survived without any lingering after effects. And as far as Luke's body? The police had taken it along with the other victims to a makeshift morgue some miles away. Before it could even be identified or listed as someone other than a refugee, Masoud's men had managed to cart off Luke's corpse before too many questions were asked.

The rest of the previous day remained a blur, beginning with their hasty dawn retreat from the camp in the company of Masoud's PKK comrades. Harper had stirred once from exhausted slumber as their driver slowed at the sight of the abandoned militia Jeep. Harper turned in her seat and met Adele's vacant gaze but nothing was said. She intermittently catnapped through the remainder of the journey, awakening once at the border cross-over into Duhok, and again as they started up the winding mountain roads.

Now, the sight of Masoud and two of his companions marching up the snowy road pulled her from these thoughts. One of them carried a couple of shovels and a pickaxe slung over his shoulder. It took Harper a moment to recognize Masoud's other companion as the young woman with the singed hair. Harper had noticed her the previous night as she attempted to console Maggie.

Adele and Maggie were still nowhere to be seen. When Masoud noticed Harper, he separated from the other two and approached the hut. He wore his arm in a sling, but otherwise seemed no worse for wear. He stopped at the edge of the stone portal and raised his good arm to indicate something in the direction of the far hillside.

"We have buried your friend," he said. "In the shadow of the mountain. Your other friend and the daughter are there." He looked away for a moment, and then nodded solemnly. "My people have a saying that a martyr never dies. He lives through us. Your friend died as much for his daughter as for my people. We are grateful and will always honor him." Then he raised his hand in a salute and walked off.

Harper began picking her way through the slushy snow in the direction Masoud had indicated. The doors of many of the houses she passed stood ajar but vacant, except for one. An ancient looking crone sat perched on a rough hewn wooden stool noting Harper's passage. She lifted her cane and shook it in a manner that Harper wanted to interpret as a salute, but guessed it was more likely mere defiance.

After a few minutes, the slushy path opened onto a small plot of level ground. Harper spotted a lone figure draped in a blanket and sitting on a pile of stones. Several dozen stone markers of various sizes arose without pattern from the grassy field. The cemetery's only other adornment was a crude obelisk topped with a small flagpole, the flag limp and unfurled in the still morning air.

It took a moment for her to realize the person seated on the pile of stones was Adele. As Harper drew near, Adele turned and glanced at her briefly before again lowering her head. Adele made a hurried sign of the cross and rose to her feet.

"Masoud has promised a headstone," she said, sniveling and wiping her eyes. "I told him I would send the money for something permanent with a suitable inscription. I have never been sentimental about gravesites, but in this instance…." She turned to Harper and smiled.

"Are you sure you don't want to arrange to have him brought home?"

"Home? Luke never had a home. We never had a home. The army life. The separations. There was never anything permanent about our lives. Surely nothing we considered a real home. Besides, Luke was a soldier. He told me once that a soldier should be buried on the battlefield where he died." She looked away and clicked her tongue in a way that sounded like disappointment. "*So gehts, ja?*. One cannot bury a memory," she said, turning back.

Harper nodded. "Where's Maggie?"

Adele shook her head.

"How is she?"

"I told you before. Maggie is resilient. She survived the orphanage." She smiled. "She survived me. At least, so far. She is brave. Like her father."

Harper placed her arm around Adele's shoulder and pulled her close. Adele responded by slipping her arm into Harper's. They stood like this for a long time before Adele pulled away. Adele swiped at her nose and took a deep breath before looking at Harper.

"The two of you never had the chance to talk, did you? You and Luke. A shame."

"I'm not sure what I would've said. These past few days I thought of so many things, none of which seemed to matter. Twenty-four years is a long time."

"*Viel Wasser unter der Brücke.* Water under the bridge," she offered.

Harper squatted in the muddy, upturned soil and laid her hand on the pile of stones that marked the grave. Someone, Adele or Maggie perhaps, had tucked a brightly colored silk scarf amongst the rocks. Harper remained like this for a long moment before rising to her feet.

"You told me once that you knew all about Sarajevo. You didn't… You couldn't know everything." She looked at Adele. "I was pregnant when I left there. I suspected it, but I didn't know for sure until the doctor at Aviano told me. He also told me it would be unlikely I'd be able to conceive again." She shook her head. "Luke never knew. Even if I would've known for sure, I doubt I would've told him. It's funny, but last week I found out that you had adopted Maggie while Luke and I were in Sarajevo together. There's something fitting, almost cosmic about that, don't you think?"

Adele took Harper's hand and squeezed it tightly. Neither of them spoke again for several minutes. Adele finally released her hand and nodded with her head in the direction of the village. Harper turned and saw Maggie strolling along the path in the company of several children. Maggie noticed them and waved before leaning down to talk to a young girl.

"What will you do now?" Harper asked.

"I am done with looking into the affairs of strangers. I will help Maggie. I believe I told you she is involved in several refugee relief organizations. Perhaps that is my calling. And you?"

"I'm not looking past Christmas with my daughter."

"And what about the story? About all this?"

"I believe I would have to be very careful and leave out certain details."

"Are you referring to my road rage?" Adele allowed herself a smile. "You should know that I did not shoot those two militiamen."

"I never thought you did."

Adele snorted. "No? Not even after you saw me shoot the one who was stealing from the refugees?"

"Well, he deserved it. Besides, that was self-defense. As for the story, there are too many angles I still need to figure out. There's the obvious question of Turkish complicity. An accusation that if I make will lend itself to a lot of scrutiny. Without some solid proof, it's pretty unlikely a story like that would see the light of day."

"I believe I know you well enough by now to know you won't forget this."

"I can only write what I can verify. And that's why there'll be a lot of questions that will go unanswered. Buried by some suck ass government appointee of some suck ass government agency. Do I sound jaded?"

"No. You're being realistic without being cynical."

"Do you think we'll ever find out why the CIA was so interested in Ozbek? The cynic in me wonders what they knew about what he was planning to do. And if they did, why didn't they do something? It's always about the crap that goes on behind closed doors, isn't it?"

Adele shrugged. "It always has been. And I suspect it always will."

"You know there are still plenty of people who would like to know about Trump's back door business deals with Erdogan. The real estate deals in Istanbul, his connections to a Turkish bank that's being investigated for money laundering. Then there's the whole stink of him giving Erdogan the green light to invade Syria and fuck over the Kurds. God, I'm ranting. This isn't the time. I'm sorry."

Adele started to say something when they heard someone beating loudly on a pan. "Breakfast, I hope," Adele said, looking up at the village.

Harper paused to glance once more at the grave before hurrying to catch up with Adele.

"You said once that when you were with Luke a little could be too much."

"And more was never enough," Adele said, finishing the thought. "That was the way it always seemed."

"Never enough." Harper grinned. "A friend of mine said she was going to engrave that on my gravestone. I keep telling myself that I've finally had enough. But then again…" She took Adele's hand and they walked up the hillside to the village.

DENNIS JUNG is the author of eight novels, three of which were selected as a finalist in the New Mexico-Arizona Book Awards. His use of visual imagery and his strong sense of place are what make his novels as much as an escape to a geographical location as the emotional landscape of his characters. Tapping into a background in anthropology, he weaves into his stories a sense of the mystical and the universal in the human experience – the drama and conflicts that consume us all, regardless of culture. Mr. Jung resides in Santa Fe, New Mexico. More about his books, including essays and excerpts, are available on his website. www.dennisjung.com